'Earth tremor!' Jamie yelled. 'And look at *that*!' he went on, just as Elaine slammed on the brakes and sent him powering towards the dashboard. His seat-belt locked and grabbed him and he was flung backwards, his head bouncing like a deranged puppet.

'Oh my . . .' he heard Elaine whisper, and when he looked up he saw a young woman dressed like a Native American Indian, running across the road. Jamie blinked and there in front of him, appearing out of the watery air, was a bearded man on horseback wearing a helmet and a metal breastplate. Reddish-gold sunlight glinted off the sword he was holding as it flashed through the air towards the young woman.

Neither of them could move. They were locked in their seats, the hushed lips of the air-conditioner blowing coolness over them, watching a horrific drama unfold. The sword swung down in a lethal arc. The girl screamed – they could hear her. The horseman moved in for the kill; there was no way he could fail . . .

FAULTLINE

FAULTLINE

GRAHAM MARKS

Catnip

CATNIP BOOKS
Published by Catnip Publishing Ltd.
Islington Business Centre
3-5 Islington High Street
London N1 9LQ

This edition published 2007
1 3 5 7 9 10 8 6 4 2

A CIP catalogue record for this book is available from the British Library

ISBN 13: 978-1-84647-023-3

Printed in Poland

www.catnippublishing.co.uk

To Daniel

Fault, *fölt* (*geol.*), a fracture or break in the earth's crust resulting in seismic movement of the rock strata, or layers, on either side – commonly called earthquakes. [Old French: *faute, falte* – Latin: *fallere*, to deceive]

San Andreas Fault, *san an-dre'as fölt*, vertical break in the earth's crust (20m/32.2km deep, 600m/965.4km long) in Calif., USA. Runs through Los Angeles in the south and San Francisco in the north; pressure build-up along the faultline can cause severe seismic tremors

CHAPTER ONE

Timeline: Wednesday, 2.15pm

The sun shone, bright in the sky. Caroline De Witt could remember the days, not so long ago, when the sky had been a rather horrible yellowy colour at this time of year and the newscasters on the radio all gave warnings about the pollution levels. Maybe there was something to be said for environmental campaigns after all – today was a beautiful day to be in the park, now that those disgusting LA smogs were almost a thing of the past.

Caroline sat, with her back against a tree and watched a scattering of kids playing on the grass, watched over by their mothers (and, because this was California, a few dads too). Although it was the holidays she knew she should have been studying – had in fact brought a couple of books with her – but it was more fun just chilling out.

At first she thought someone's dog must have been trying to chase a cat or something. The shrill, high-pitched noise seemed to come from a very long way away, a couple of hundred metres off to her left and behind a small shrub-covered rise. Caroline frowned as she looked over that way, wondering what was going on; no-one else seemed to have heard anything.

She picked up her sunglasses and put them on in order to see better into the sun, and thought that it was odd the way the air at the centre of the rise looked like it was boiling; it was hot, but not hot enough, yet, for that kind of ripple effect. The sound of a child crying made her look away. No big deal, just a teddy bear ownership upset, but when she looked back something had changed.

There was an animal, a big animal, running down the slope into the open parkland. For a moment Caroline thought it was a kangaroo, but then it occurred to her that kangaroos don't run, they hop – and anyway, the nearest zoo was in Griffith Park, and that was miles away, so a kangaroo wasn't very likely. She leaned forward, shading her eyes, and squinted to try and get a clearer idea of what she was looking at and then she noticed that, whatever the creature was, it was obviously hurt and in trouble.

Before she had a chance to be surprised that it was also light green with vivid blue stripes running down its side, she saw three more creatures, much smaller ones, come tearing over the slope after it.

Caroline stood up. There was something very, very wrong here, but she couldn't work out what it was; fascinated and scared at the same time, her eyes stayed fixed on the drama unfolding in front of her. She could hear that other people in the park had also spotted something was up – adult voices were calling for children to come to them – and she knew she herself should probably run, but all she did was get closer to the tree.

The three smaller creatures, all of them making a weird chittering sound, then leapt on the big animal and started attacking it ferociously. The big animal screamed and blood sprayed, like a lazy fountain, into the air. It was like watching one of those documentaries on TV where some poor antelope gets taken out by a pack of hyenas. Only on TV they showed the whole thing in slow-motion – here in the park it was all real-time. Extremely fast, very real time.

Caroline could feel her heart pounding, fear rising as she watched the horrific sight, her mind still not able to make any sense of what she was seeing. These animals looked incredibly familiar, yet at the same time totally unreal, and the violence and savagery of the fight was so intense it was staggering to watch.

And then from somewhere over to her right she saw a young boy come riding on his bicycle. He must have been nine or ten years old, dressed in bright coloured shorts and a white T-shirt, his long bleach-blond hair flying out behind him.

She saw him skid to a halt, staring open-mouthed at the bloody tangle of claws, flesh and teeth twenty or so metres in front of him . . .

She saw one of the smaller creatures stop what it was doing and jerk its tiny, elongated head his way . . .

She saw it leap off the flailing body it was standing on and start running towards the boy . . .

Caroline tried to scream, but nothing seemed to work. The boy took one look at the compact, almost lizard-like thing scything his way and began frantically pedalling, his rear wheel throwing up bits of grass. But he was too slow. As Caroline finally managed to get her feet to do what she told them and started running, she saw the creature launch itself through the air. The boy didn't have a chance.

By now the whole park was in total uproar, but above it all Caroline heard someone yelling something about getting back, keeping away, and the next thing she knew shots were ringing out.

Gunfire was something everybody assumed somebody living in Los Angeles would be very familiar with, but outside of cop shows on TV, Caroline had never actually heard it before. It was loud, but in a dull, thudding kind of way, and she heard it like a drum beat – *BAM! BE-BAM-BAM-BAM!* – four shots in quick succession.

The creature attacking the boy appeared to be hit by an invisible punch, its head flung sideways as a bullet exploded through and out of its skull, and then it stopped moving; a hurried glance told her the rest of the creatures had also been shot. Caroline realized she was shaking uncontrollably and that her face was wet with tears. A nice quiet afternoon in the park had turned into a waking nightmare of loud, red death.

'Are you OK? Are you hurt?'

Caroline looked round to see a man standing next to her. He wore a white short-sleeved shirt with a couple of ball-points in the pocket and looked like a shoe salesman, except he was holding a large gun that still had a wisp of blue smoke trailing out of its barrel.

'I'm fine . . . really, I'm OK,' she said, wiping her face with the back of her hand. 'What . . . ?'

'I got no idea,' said the man, shaking his head. 'I was just having my lunch over there,' he waved behind him, 'heard all the commotion and came round the trees to see this butcher's shop— Did you see what happened, how it started?'

'All I saw was this big animal come running over the hill, and then the three smaller ones came after it . . . and then . . .' the tears started coming again as she remembered,' . . . and then the boy . . .'

'It's over now,' said the man. 'My partner's radioed in for help . . . ambulances and stuff . . . we should move back, not touch anything.'

'But what about the boy?' Caroline looked over her shoulder and saw another man, also with a gun in his hand, standing with a small group of parents and children. 'Shouldn't we see if . . .'

'Even from here I can tell there's no point,' said the man. 'Come on, let's get back with the others. We'll have to take statements and details from all of you.'

'What can *I* tell you?' Caroline almost shouted, anger rising as her fear ebbed away. 'I don't know what those things are, *I* don't know where they came from any more than *you* do!'

'But it's my job to find out, miss,' said the man, calmly, putting his arm out to usher her down the slope. 'I'm a policeman, a detective, it's what I do . . . ask questions and look for answers.'

'I'm sorry for shouting,' said Caroline, sniffing. In the distance she could hear the mournful wail of sirens. Lots of sirens. 'I'm upset . . . those things, it was so horrible – what could they possibly be?'

'Apart from dead, I've no idea, miss,' said the detective, putting his gun back in the leather holster clipped to the back of his belt. 'My kid was watching the DVD of *Jurassic Park* last week and, if I didn't know any better, I'd've said they were dinosaurs . . .'

CHAPTER TWO

Timeline: Wednesday, 2.45pm

The air-conditioning in the *Post-Register*'s offices wasn't cranked up very high for two reasons: it wasn't really hot enough outside, but mainly the machinery was far too old and decrepit to take the strain. The summer, when it arrived, was going to be murder.

This time in the afternoon was always pretty slow. The evening deadline was hours away and the only people really working were the feature writers whose stories weren't tied to the push and shove of the news pages. Reporters looked down on the men and women of the Features Department – they had no idea, so the feeling went, what was meant by pressure.

At the News Desk, actually an untidy collection of a dozen or so old wooden desks all littered with paper, screens, keyboards and half-drunk cups of cold machine-made coffee, sat three people: Tony Stone, the *Post*'s Science Editor, Elaine McFarlane, who covered crime, and Jamie Delgado, a sixteen-year-old who wanted to be a journalist when he left college and whose father was an old buddy and golfing partner of the paper's owner.

As long as he didn't get in the way, and he didn't complain about getting coffee and doughnuts whenever he was asked, Jamie was more than tolerated by the news team. An unpaid slave was a definite bonus to office life. On the other hand, Jamie loved being there – what better way could there be to spend your holidays than in the middle of something as intense as a newspaper?

Even when nothing was happening it was interesting listening to the reporters talking about past triumphs, great jokes they'd played on colleagues on other papers and what a bunch of time-wasters most TV people were.

Elaine, a noisy thirty-something blonde originally from somewhere around Chicago, was leaning back in her chair and throwing scrunched up pieces of paper into a nearby bin – and mostly missing. She was telling Tony about a cop she'd heard was suing a local Mexican restaurant for causing 'actual physical harm' because it had put too much chilli powder in a dip it had labelled 'mild' when the phone went.

'News desk,' said Tony, picking up the phone as it was right next to him and then listening. 'For you,' he said, waving the receiver at Elaine. 'Something about a shooting in a park out in the Valley.'

Elaine grounded her chair and punched a button on her phone. 'McFarlane here,' she said. 'Who'm I talking to?'

Jamie watched as she nodded and took quick shorthand notes on the pad she always kept within easy grabbing distance. 'Who got shot?' he asked Tony.

'Dunno,' he shrugged. 'Some kid, I think . . . the caller was a little incoherent.'

'Was it a drive-by?'

'Don't think so, not gang territory,' said Tony. 'Maybe a domestic – we'll find out soon enough, she's coming off the phone . . .'

'I owe you one, Dave,' Elaine said to her caller, cutting the line and immediately redialling.

'What's happening?' asked Tony.

'Major incident in some park out in Tarzana . . . whole place cordoned off.' Elaine frowned, standing up and grabbing her bag as she waited for the phone to be answered. 'Apparently more cops out there than on a St Patrick's Day parade and my car's in the— Julio? Hi, Elaine, is the Honda ready yet? It is, right, I'll be down.'

'Can I come with you, Elaine?' asked Jamie, mentally crossing his fingers; this sounded like a biggie and he really wanted to go. 'I've got film in my camera . . .'

Elaine looked at him, thought for a moment and then nodded. 'OK,' she said, 'but stay with me and do *exactly* what I tell you.'

'Great!' Jamie punched the air and went to get his camera bag.

'It's like having a excitable Labrador pup around the place,' said Elaine. 'Except he hasn't got a tail to wag.'

'He's OK,' grinned Tony, 'for the son of a friend of the boss . . . could've been a heck of a lot worse – remember that kid we had in here a couple of years ago? Did nothing but complain all the time?'

'Yeah, Jamie's all right,' Elaine turned her monitor off and picked up her mobile phone. 'Tell Henry – *when* he gets back from his executive lunch – to save me some space on the front page . . . I've got a feeling about this story.'

Tony watched her as she walked out, Jamie following her. She was right; if Jamie had had a tail it would have been going nineteen to the dozen right now. He also thought she was probably right about the story; Elaine had what they called in the business a good nose for stories and he wondered what she'd find out about this particular one.

Technically he was part of the features team, but only because the editor had one day insisted they needed a Science correspondent and had made him it as he was a physics graduate – which in Henry's eyes made him the perfect choice to do the job. Tony sighed and got up. He supposed he'd better get back to work.

CHAPTER THREE

Timeline: Wednesday, 11.20pm

The fluorescent strips in the morgue seemed to radiate cold as well as light, and they made everyone look ill – especially the dead people. The small group of men standing in a huddle down one end of the white tiled room looked worried, each of them casting hurried glances at the three stainless steel tables and wheeled trolley standing a couple of metres away from them.

There were unidentifiable *things* lying on the tables and the trolley, each object covered by a sheet with dark stains on it, and from one table – the one with the biggest thing on it – what looked like a long, light green snake with blue markings trailed to the floor. There was also a curious smell in the air that the extractor fans and disinfectant couldn't seem to get rid of.

The post mortems were over – the boy's had been done in a separate room – and the men, a collection of high-ranking police officers, health officials and politicians, were waiting for the chief pathologist to come back after cleaning up.

The whole building had been closed off and no-one was saying anything to anyone; a short, five-line press release had been given out late in the afternoon, stating that the incident in the park had been caused by a pack of wild, feral dogs, and that was all the information the outside world had been given. And as everyone in the room knew, it was about as far from the truth as it was possible to get.

The door swung open and the chief pathologist walked in, her assistant following her. They were both wearing clean white coats.

'Gentlemen,' she said, pausing until she had everyone's attention. 'While I was out the test results came through and we had a fax from the Smithsonian Museum as well . . . I know you're going to find this as hard to believe as I do, but *everything* confirms my first suspicions.'

'But it's just not possible!' a grey-haired man with a rather unhealthy, flushed complexion snorted.

'We're not here to decide what's possible and not possible, Commissioner,' said a younger man whose steel-rimmed glasses made him look like a hawk. 'We're here to look at Dr Weiss's information and decide what to do next, how we're going to handle this thing.'

'Don't try and teach me my job, Hardiman,' said the Police Commissioner angrily.

'Do you want to know the details,' interrupted Dr Weiss, 'or do you just want to carry on bickering?'

'Our apologies, Sandra . . . it's been a stressful afternoon, to say the least,' said Hardiman. 'Give us the low-down.'

Sandra Weiss turned to her assistant and took the folder he was holding. She opened it and scanned the three or four flimsy sheets of paper it contained and then took her glasses off.

'All four creatures,' she indicated the tables and the trolley, 'are what can loosely be termed dinosaurs . . .' The group in front of her collectively shook their heads and shuffled their feet, watching as she walked over to the nearest table and pulled back the sheet.

'This one, the largest of the four, is, I am reliably informed, what the experts call a herbivorous ornithopod named *Tenatosaurus*. Tests show that its stomach contents are made up of extinct plant and vegetable matter, and I'm told it's a young male.' She drew the sheet back over the creature and walked to the next table.

'The three other creatures are all the same type – a hunter-killer known as *Dienonychus*.' She paused, took a deep breath, and continued. 'They all lived some one hundred million years ago in the Cretaceous period, and like it or not, gentlemen, those are the indisputable facts. The ball, as far as *I'm* concerned, is now firmly back in your court.'

No-one spoke for quite some time and everyone appeared to be very interested in the state of their shoes.

'So there's no chance these things escaped from somewhere – they're not some studio special effect?' said the Commissioner, breaking the awkward silence.

'No chance at all,' replied Sandra Weiss. 'If you think I'm making all this stuff up, come and take a *really* close look at what's under these sheets – or would you rather go next door and see what one of them did to that kid?'

The Commissioner shook his head and turned to Hardiman. 'So what's the Governor's Office going to do about this? We *can't* let the story out – it could cause almost more trouble than the darned earthquake . . . I mean, prehistoric *monsters* running around all over the place, killing kids!'

Before Hardiman had a chance to speak, a man poked his head round the door to the morgue and beckoned to him. 'Excuse me a moment,' he said and hurriedly left the room.

The Commissioner turned to the person next to him. 'What's happening outside, Karl?'

'Last report was that most of the media types had got bored and gone home, sir,' said the man. 'Nothing's happened, there's nothing to see . . . also, a big fire broke out at about five, near the Santa Monica Airport and all the TV trucks and crews left to go cover that for the six o'clock news.'

'Every smoke cloud has a silver lining,' remarked someone, and a couple of people laughed nervously.

There was no doubt in anyone's mind that the problem they were faced with could hardly be bigger. Somehow, in the middle of one of the largest cities in the world, four *actual* dinosaurs had appeared out of nowhere and killed a ten-year-old boy. The incident had been witnessed by a couple of dozen members of the public – admittedly some half of them children under the age of five – and two off-duty LAPD detectives. Stopping this particular cat from getting out of the bag wasn't going to be easy. If the truth became a matter of public knowledge . . . well, they'd just have to keep their fingers crossed it never happened.

The door opened and Hardiman walked back in, followed by a newcomer who was carrying a slim leather briefcase. 'This is Gene Cardwell,' said Hardiman. 'He's in charge now.'

'In charge of what?' blustered the Commissioner.

'Everything,' said Cardwell; his voice sounded harsh and gritty and had the kind of tone that said he meant business. 'Most of you probably haven't heard of the Special Scientific Office,' he went on, 'but we're a federal agency with full powers, granted by the President, to do what we like where we like – and here are the papers that say so, Commissioner,' he said, taking a white envelope out of his inside jacket pocket and handing it over.

The Commissioner took it and was about to speak when he saw the Presidential seal. Instead, he handed the envelope back. 'I've got no problem with your taking over, Mr Cardwell,' he said, smiling like a wily fox. 'In fact I'm glad someone's taking full responsibility for this mess . . . are you going to tell us what you're going to do?'

'Yes,' said Cardwell, opening his case. 'For a start, you're all about to sign a document that states you won't say one word to anyone about anything that's happened today.'

'Or else?' said the Commissioner.

'Or else you go to prison,' said Cardwell. 'Anyone need a pen?'

Steve Hardiman watched Cardwell check all the papers had been completed properly and put them in his briefcase. He'd first met the man a couple of weeks ago when he'd arrived from Washington, with what he liked to call his 'task force', to investigate the rash of weirdness in the state. Steve had been assigned the job of liaison between the SSO and the Governor, but all that had meant was him acting as nothing more than a glorified run-around.

'So,' said Steve, 'd'you think you've got the lid tight enough on this one, Gene?'

'Yup,' came the terse reply. Cardwell, thought Steve, didn't just play at being tough, he lived the part completely. Never gave anything away.

'Any more info about what Whelan's doing poking his nose into things?'

'Whelan's an irritation, but he's not a problem,' said Cardwell, locking his briefcase. 'In fact he's even more paranoid about publicity than we are . . . and the guy he's got running things here, Charles Dobson, he's ex-CIA, a real pro. All we have to do is keep an eye on them; we can close them down any time we have to. There are other things going on at the moment that are *far* more disturbing than whatever Cletus Whelan's up to . . .'

CHAPTER FOUR

Timeline: Wednesday, 11.45pm

Jamie sat in his bedroom staring at his TV, which was tuned to a local twenty-four-hour news station. Elaine had dropped him at his house at around eight o'clock and then gone back to the office. It had been a frustrating afternoon all round; by the time they'd got to the place – somewhere called Serrania Park – all there was to see was a large crowd of people at the entrance being held back by almost as many police.

They'd checked every possible point of entry, but the park was sealed up tighter than a vacuum-packed portion of cheese. There was no way in, and as far as anyone could tell, anything coming out was making the journey by helicopter. Some time about five in the afternoon word reached the increasingly frantic pack of journalists that the action appeared to have moved to the County Morgue.

It had been like the start of a Le Mans race; everyone tearing off to their car, the air filled with the squeal of tyres, angry honking of horns and clouds of exhaust fumes. But if anything it was even more boring at the morgue. Jamie had been sent by Elaine to get urgently needed supplies of coffee and doughnuts and that was about the most excitement he'd had.

In front of him he had a copy of the press release a flustered secretary had passed out at about six-thirty. He read it again:

as of 17.00 hours today, the lapd are still unable to give any more details of the event that took place this afternoon in serrania park, tarzana, except to confirm there has been one fatality from what is thought to have been an attack by a number of feral or wild dogs.

It didn't sound any more convincing now than it had the first time he'd read it. If it was only wild dogs – and Jamie had heard that, along with coyotes, packs of abandoned dogs did roam all round Los Angeles – why were the police being so mysterious about things?

Elaine had found out that all the witnesses, including the cops, had been whisked away to some unspecified hospital for 'special counselling' to get over the shock of what they'd seen. And that was *all* she'd managed to find out, which had made her even more suspicious because, as she'd said while she drove him home, people who'd been involved in real gun battles hardly got more than a cup of coffee and a Kleenex from the medics these days.

She'd left him by his front gate, muttering something about cover-ups and conspiracies, and had roared off down the road, her mobile phone tucked under her ear. Jamie had felt let down and sort of rejected as he'd watched her car disappear; going home was no substitute for being in the middle of a real-life drama, and it was moments like these that made him hate being his age and wish that he were old enough to control his life. But that wasn't going to happen for a few years yet.

For now all he could do was wait until tomorrow morning when he could get back into the thick of things. It was nearly midnight and the house was silent; his parents were still out at some charity event and his older sister had gone to bed ages ago. He wondered about calling the *Post* to see if Elaine was still there, whether anything else had happened, but thought better of it. The last major news round-up on TV, leading with something about an earth tremor out in the Valley, hadn't even mentioned the story – it was as though it hadn't ever happened – but, if there was anything new to know, tomorrow would be soon enough.

As he brushed his teeth he noticed a couple of spots on his forehead and what looked like the start of one on his cheek. He was seriously going to have to cut down on the junk food, though hanging round with the likes of Elaine and Tony would make that almost impossible.

Far from calming down at this time of night, every floor at the *Post* blazed with light. The first edition was about to start printing, and now was the time, if you had to do it, to shout '*Hold the front page!*'.

The minute hand on the clock near the News Desk clicked round closer and closer to twelve-fifteen, the time Henry, the editor, would phone down to the basement and set the presses rolling. When he did, the whole building would begin to fill with a deep bass hum and seem to shake until the huge machines settled into the relentless rhythm that turned what looked like vast toilet rolls into tomorrow's newspapers.

Elaine sat at her desk. It was a complete mess: yellow stick-it notes waved tiredly at her from all round the monitor, a regiment of half-empty cups of coffee stood ready to obey orders to leap into the rubbish bin, but would have to wait because that was already full to overflowing, and she couldn't see her phone at all. But Elaine didn't care.

She was exhausted and completely ticked off. All her hard work had resulted in a half-page somewhere inside the paper, no picture. What was the point of giving it more? Henry had said. And no matter how much she wanted to say otherwise, she couldn't disagree with him; the story had gone nowhere – a spectacular dead-end that had had all the signs of being something to run with.

'You look all-in,' said a voice.

Elaine looked up, rubbed her eyes and focused on Tony, standing across the desk from her. 'Just waiting for my second wind to kick in,' she replied, smiling weakly.

'I've been doing a bit of digging of my own,' Tony sat down opposite her. 'Want to hear what I've got?'

'As long as it's not a sighting of Elvis in Serrania Park, yes.'

Tony leaned forward and almost whispered: 'Giant lizards.'

'Giant *lizards*!'

'Quiet!' hissed Tony. 'This is *very* unofficial, Elaine . . . I had to pull in some major favours on this one. Let's go outside where the air is fresher and it's a little more private.'

Elaine followed him down the stairs and out into the car park. The colder air cleared her head and she didn't say anything until Tony sat down on a low wall. 'So,' she nodded at him, 'you were saying?'

'Back when I was just a mere reporter, and not the *Post*'s answer to Albert Einstein, I had a contact at the County Morgue,' explained Tony. 'He used to provide me with information, and in return I kept quiet about certain of his out-of-hours activities that I happened to have found out about.'

'I won't ask.'

'Don't let your imagination run away with you, it wasn't anything gruesome,' Tony smiled. 'Anyway, I tracked him down again and put a bit of pressure on him.'

'I've never thought of you as the threatening type, Tony.'

'I'm just *very* persuasive, Elaine.'

'So, don't keep me hanging on – what did he tell you?'

'Basically that the "pack of dogs" press release is a fairy tale,' said Tony.

'I hope you didn't pay good money for that information – even Jamie took one look at it and knew straight off it was about as accurate as a sundial in a rain storm.'

'He said the unofficial word was that there are four very large, very dead reptiles under heavy guard at the morgue,' Tony carried on, 'or, to use his more colourful phrase, "a buncha humungous lizards, man!", and he said the place was heaving with what he called spooks.'

'Spooks?' frowned Elaine. 'Did he mean CIA?'

'I asked that and he just said that the whole basement area, where the cold rooms are, was out of bounds to all staff,' said Tony, standing up and stretching. 'Out of bounds and guarded by guys with little ear-plugs and big bulges under their arms. Oh yeah, and he'd been made to sign a piece of paper that means if they find out he's talked he's in serious trouble.'

'I *knew* there was a cover-up – just *knew* it! So why did he?'

'Why did he what?'

'Talk, Tony,' said Elaine. 'Why did he talk?'

'He doesn't scare easily and, more importantly, he hates being told what to do.' Tony turned and looked up at the building.' . . . And I promised him we wouldn't print the story.'

'You did *what*!' Elaine almost shouted. 'So why are you telling me if I can't use the darn information?'

'Because I knew you were right, there was definitely a story there,' said Tony. 'And I could see you weren't getting anywhere. I thought that if I could get some confirmation you were on the right track you'd carry on looking.'

'You think I'm a quitter, Tony?'

'No, but I think Henry'll *make* you quit if you don't get a break soon.'

'I think you're right,' Elaine punched him lightly on the arm. 'Sorry for losing it back there, and thanks for helping . . . it's good to know I wasn't barking completely up the wrong tree.'

'Except you still don't know what that tree looks like.'

'True,' said Elaine, 'but a tiny thought has just sprouted roots, and with a little watering, it might just become a big thought.'

'And what is that thought?' asked Tony, as they started walking back into the building.

'What if this isn't the first time it's happened?'

CHAPTER FIVE

Timeline: Thursday, 9.00am

Jamie walked into the office feeling like a pack animal on a Rocky Mountain trek. His camera bag was slung over one shoulder, he had a parcel that had been left at the front desk for Elaine tucked under his arm, and he was carrying a cardboard tray piled up with a selection of Danish pastries. His first job every morning was a trip to the local deli. Sometimes, he thought, it just wasn't worth trying to save time and effort.

Hardly anyone was in the office and the news desk was empty – empty of people, anyway. Otherwise it looked like a paper bomb had exploded with devastating effect. Jamie was clearing a space on the desk that he now thought of as 'his' when he saw Elaine coming out of the lift. She looked like she'd slept in her clothes.

'Hi,' he said, wondering what on earth she'd been up to. 'Someone left a package for you, it's on your desk.'

'You haven't touched anything, have you?'

'I wouldn't dare.'

'Sorry, Jamie, didn't mean to snap,' Elaine blew a wisp of hair out of her face. 'I've been up all night, literally.'

'Doing what?'

'Research, young man.' She sat down the way a heavy

bag of shopping does, groaning. 'Research, the meat and potatoes of a journalist's diet, the bones you build a story out of – or at least try to – if I'm allowed to mix my metaphors.'

'Which story?'

'The Serrania Park Mystery, what else?' she reached over and hooked the stickiest pastry on the tray. 'Sugar overload, exactly what this body needs right now.'

'Did you find anything?' asked Jamie.

'I *found* lots of things,' Elaine waved the pastry at her desk, 'but I don't know if any of it means anything.'

'Can I help?'

'You sure can, Jamie.' She held up a sheaf of papers – print-outs, faxes and scribbled notes. 'While I zip home, have a shower and change into some clothes that don't itch so much, you can start going through these.'

'And doing what with them?'

'What's left of my brain tells me that somewhere in there there's a pattern,' said Elaine, slowly standing up. 'And once we find the pattern we can start making a picture . . . so start thinking laterally, Jamie.'

'Huh?' Jamie looked puzzled.

'Don't think in straight lines,' explained Elaine as she searched for her car keys. 'Look *around* things, look sideways, turn things upside down – the world doesn't run on rails.'

'Are we talking Chaos Theory here?'

'Kind of,' said Elaine, finally locating her keys. 'Strange things happen, but they rarely happen in isolation, all on their own. There's always a reason, and we just have to find it . . . cos without one, we ain't got no story.'

'Shall I open the package?'

'No,' Elaine shook her head, 'there's enough stuff to deal with without adding to your problems.'

'See you later, then,' said Jamie, staring at her desk.

'Think of it as creative filing . . .'

And, in a manner of speaking, it was. Jamie started the only place he could, at the top of the avalanche, and began to work his way down. The papers seemed to fall into four types: photostats from the *Post*'s own back-issue files, faxes from other newspapers and news organizations, copies of articles from books and magazines, and computer print-outs of stuff Elaine had obviously downloaded from the Internet.

Sorting the one big pile into a few smaller ones was the easy bit; once he'd done that Jamie was faced with the problem of what to do next. At first none of the stories and snippets of information seemed to have any connection with each other, except that they were all very weird – as weird, in their own way, as what had happened yesterday in the park. And that's when a lightbulb went on over Jamie's head.

He went to the stationery cupboard and got a fistful of different coloured stickers and a box of paper-clips. Articles and stories about anything to do with UFOs got a yellow sticker, ghosts and apparitions a blue one, unexplained happenings a green one and so on, until

Elaine's desk was covered in loads of very tidy piles of paper. If there was a pattern it wasn't anything quite so obvious as polka dot or paisley, and he couldn't see it at all.

As he was working his way through everything, Tony, whom Jamie hadn't noticed arrive, came over to the desk.

'Any idea where Elaine is?' he asked.

'She went home to shower and change,' said Jamie, looking at his watch. 'She left about nine-thirty . . . it's nearly eleven now, so I expect she'll be here soon – can I help?'

'Not really,' said Tony, pulling his lower lip and frowning. 'I need to speak to her. I'll try and get her on her mobile number.'

'She left it behind,' said Jamie, picking up the small black phone, its tiny green light cheerfully winking away and telling anyone who cared that it was ready and willing to dial the world. 'It was under all the papers.'

'Rats!' scowled Tony. 'I hope she isn't too long . . .'

'What's happened?' said Elaine.

Jamie and Tony had their backs to the lifts and hadn't seen her come into the office; they both whirled round.

'Somebody die?' she asked.

'No,' said Tony, 'somebody disappeared.'

'Who?' queried Elaine, looking at her desk and smiling at Jamie.

'My contact at the . . . ah . . . at the morgue . . .'

Elaine sat down. 'Tell all,' she said.

In a hushed voice Tony explained that, first thing that morning, he'd called his man at home to assure him nothing he'd said would be printed but he couldn't get a reply. Thinking this was a bit odd, his man not being known as an early riser, Tony had gone round before coming to work.

'His place was locked up tight,' he said, 'and while I was knocking on the back door, a neighbour came out and told me he'd gone on a month's holiday.'

'So he hasn't disappeared,' said Elaine.

'He's only just got back from a three-week trip to Mexico, Elaine . . . and he told me that was his holiday for the year,' Tony scratched his head absentmindedly. 'Something's happened to him – I think they, whoever "they" are, found out he'd talked.'

'And I thought *I* was the conspiracy nut-case around here,' said Elaine, aware that Jamie was staring at them both with his mouth open. 'I see you've been busy, Jamie.'

'Uh, yeah,' he said. 'Sort of makes sense now, kind of.'

'Well I'm glad something does,' said Tony, getting up. 'Whatever it is you're getting yourself into, Elaine, be careful.'

'You know me, Tony,' she replied.

'Exactly,' nodded Tony, walking back to his desk.

Elaine and Jamie spent the rest of the morning going over everything he'd done, entering it all on to a new database file. Jamie still couldn't figure out what the pattern was until Elaine pointed out that all the stories she'd collected, odd, weird and strange as they were, had no satisfactory ending and had been left, like untied shoelaces, hanging.

'Did you notice anything else?' asked Elaine, as she furiously attacked the helpless keyboard, pummelling the last of the information into the computer.

'Like what?' asked Jamie. He was beginning to feel hungry, and all there was left to eat was half a stale pastry.

'The dates . . . look at the dates.'

Jamie scanned the clipped piles of paper, trying to see what Elaine had seen. 'Well . . .' he said eventually, 'all I can say is that there's been a lot more stuff going on in the last few weeks . . .'

'On the button!' grinned Elaine, pushing her chair back and flexing her hands.

'What d'you mean?'

'Something's going on and it's building up.' Elaine nodded at the screen. 'I can't pinpoint when it all started, but California has been experiencing something of an epidemic of the bizarre, far beyond what even this town considers normal!'

'What are you going to do?'

'Let's play with the database for a bit.' Elaine leaned over and tapped a couple of keys. The screen blanked for a second, the information rearranged itself into date order and Elaine printed it out. She then got it by county and finally, using a special scale she'd attached to each entry, in order of weirdness.

And there was the pattern. A slow but steady increase in reports of stories that – like the Serrania Park incident – went off like a damp firework. Lots of promise, but no bang.

Elaine sat for some time, chewing on a pencil and sifting through the lists. 'OK,' she said at last, 'let's do lunch.'

'Is that it?' said Jamie, who'd been expecting something more.

'And then we go and do a bit of digging.'

'We?' grinned Jamie.

'Unless you'd rather stay here of course . . .'

CHAPTER SIX

Timeline: Thursday, 2.35pm

Lunch had been a hot dog and a milkshake in Elaine's car. While she was driving. Life in the fast lane, thought Jamie.

'Where are we going?' he asked as he stuffed his paper napkin into the door pocket. It wasn't, he noticed, going to be lonely.

'We're working our way out of town, up the I-5,' replied Elaine, 'checking out a couple or three of the nearest oddball news reports.'

'We're not going to Sacremento, are we?'

'Not quite, but we could be a tad late getting back,' Elaine said. 'D'you want to call your mum and let her know'

'I . . . um . . .'

'What?'

'I forgot to charge my phone up,' Jamie shrugged, embarrassed; some hot-shot reporter he'd turned out to be. 'Battery's flat . . .'

'No worries,' Elaine dug her phone out of her handbag. 'Use mine.'

Their first stop had been at a shopping mall where a

guard had reported seeing what he said looked just like a marauding band of cowboys firing their pistols and riding hell-for-leather *through* the shops on the ground floor. A number of alarms had gone off, bringing a cavalry charge of police out to the mall, but they could find no sign of forced entry, not least by a person or persons on horseback.

It had happened at about two in the morning, with only low-level security lighting on, but the guard had sworn he wasn't making it all up. Tests proved he hadn't been drinking, but his company thought it wise to put him back on day shifts anyway – which was why Jamie and Elaine found him trying to explain to an old lady that he wasn't a *real* policeman and therefore couldn't arrest a small boy for sticking his tongue out at her.

He was only too glad to talk about what had happened that night, especially to people who appeared to believe he wasn't mad.

'They was *there*!' said the guard, whose plastic identity badge said his parents had thought it a neat idea to christen him Tanquerey ('Call me Tank') McFadden. 'I saw them and I *heard* them and there was stuff on the floor after they'd gone, too.'

'What stuff?' asked Elaine.

'Dirt,' said Tank, 'and scratches on the marble from all the damn horseshoes.'

'Can you show us the scratches?' said Elaine.

'The clean-up guys got rid of everything,' said Tank. 'When I came back on duty – the company made me take a coupla days off, sayin' I was probly sufferin' from overwork, which I wasn't – there was no sign, not a one, to show what had happened . . . but what I can't figure is that it must've been caught on the video, those cameras run twenty-four hours, seven days a week.'

'And?' prompted Elaine.

'And no-one's ever said a word about it.'

Thanking the guard for his time, Elaine made some calls and discovered that – surprise, surprise – the video recording of that particular night had been misplaced and couldn't be viewed. She also found out that a different cleaning company from the normal one had turned up, very early, and cleaned the mall from top to bottom.

One shop owner, who'd seen their vans leaving as he came to work and taken their number, had been so impressed by the job they'd done he'd rung them to try and get them to quote for becoming the regular firm. The number he'd taken down didn't exist, and he couldn't find a record of them anywhere. It was odd, he thought, but maybe they'd gone out of business.

On their way out of the mall (or the Cedar-Pines Shopping Village, as it liked to be known), Tank came running after them. He'd remembered something, he said; a man had been round to his house, one of the days he'd been off, asking questions. He'd left a card, in case Tank had got any more information for him, and had said he was particularly interested in any objects that might have escaped the clean-up guys.

'What was his name?' asked Elaine.

'Denton, or Dodgeson – I can't exactly remember,' Tank

shook his head. 'And I left the card at home . . . didn't have an address, just a phone number, mobile I think.'

'Did you call him?'

'No point,' said Tank. 'That place was so spick and span you could've eaten your lunch off the floor.'

'Well, thanks anyway.' Elaine reached out, shook Tank's hand and then gave him her own card. 'If he gets in touch again, would you let me know?'

'Be a pleasure, ma'am,' grinned Tank.

It was now five-thirty and they were on their way back to Los Angeles from their last call. Jamie was beginning to wonder if the whole world wasn't going completely crazy. They'd spoken to a woman who claimed to have seen – in broad daylight – a man dressed in very dirty, old-fashioned clothes, and carrying what she described as 'gold-mining stuff', walk across her living room and through the wall. She'd had to get the hoover out and vacuum the place as he'd left a trail of mud behind him.

She also told them that, after the report appeared in the newspaper, she'd been visited by a couple of people from some government agency she couldn't remember the name of, who ('Now isn't this real strange?' she'd said) wanted to know if she still had the dust bag from the vacuum cleaner. When they found she'd thrown it away they'd gone and hadn't left a card or anything, but the other person had. Elaine now had the phone number and the name of the mysterious visitor. It was a Mr Charles Dobson.

He had also visited the other two places on Elaine's list. The first was a man who'd gone into his garage to find what he called 'semi-naked cavemen' skinning some kind of big cat with very large teeth; when he'd come back (with his gun, naturally), they'd disappeared leaving only a pool of blood and bits of fur on the concrete. He'd got his high-pressure hose out and sluiced the whole place down.

The second was a family called Fraser whose five-year-old boy had insisted he'd spent the morning watching pirates dig up the back garden of an empty neighbouring house. When his parents had gone to have a look, sure enough, there was a hole, a lot of strange grey dust – even some gold coins – but no pirates. That nice Mr Dobson, who'd arrived a couple of hours before the rather nastier government people, had bought the coins for a lot of money. Cash. The parents refused to say how much.

'This has been the most bizarre day of my life,' said Jamie, popping a second can of soda and handing that one to Elaine. 'What the heck is going on?'

'I don't know, Jamie,' she replied. 'But it looks like there are folks out there who know a lot more than we do. What did Mr Fraser say that agency was called?'

'Let me look.' Jamie got out the pad he'd been using to take notes while Elaine talked to people and flicked through the pages until he came to what he wanted. 'Mr Fraser thought the man's badge had said something like Special Scientific Office – have you ever heard of them?'

'Never,' said Elaine, 'but as soon as I get back to the paper I'm going to check them out – *and* our Mr Dobson.'

'What d'you think he's up to?'

'Good question.' Elaine drained the can and threw it behind her. 'He only left calling cards if he got to places *after* the SSO types, so you've got to figure he's not keen on them knowing how to get hold of him . . . As to what he's up to, he sounds like some rich nut who collects things, though why he has to be so secretive about it is anyone's guess.'

The sun was starting its daily suicide dive for the horizon, which was already bleeding with anticipation. For no good reason, except she liked it, Elaine had chosen to take the scenic route home and they were meandering along a small dusty road. To Jamie's left were open fields and scrub-covered brush; to his right, some few hundred metres away, were the low hills towards which the sun was making. Straight ahead, but out of sight, was the teeming ant-hill that was Los Angeles.

He was just about to ask Elaine if he could phone home again and let his mum know he was all right when he noticed something strange. The road in front seemed to start shaking, Elaine grabbing the wheel as the Honda veered off course, and about thirty metres in front and to the right of the car Jamie could swear he saw a wide column of shimmering liquid air.

'Earth tremor!' Jamie yelled. 'And look at *that*!' he went on, just as Elaine slammed on the brakes and sent him powering towards the dashboard. His seat-belt locked and grabbed him and he was flung backwards, his head bouncing like a deranged puppet.

'Oh my . . .' he heard Elaine whisper, and when he looked up he saw a young woman dressed like a Native American Indian, running across the road. Jamie blinked and there in front of him, appearing out of the watery air, was a bearded man on horseback wearing a helmet and metal breastplate. Reddish-gold sunlight glinted off the sword he was holding as it flashed through the air towards the young woman.

Neither of them could move. They were locked in their seats, the hushed lips of the air-conditioner blowing coolness over them, watching a horrific drama unfold. The sword swung down in a lethal arc. The girl screamed – they could hear her. The horseman moved in for the kill; there was no way he could fail . . .

And then, as suddenly as it had all started, the violent image vanished – almost evaporated in front of them.

Elaine broke the spell, stabbing at her seat-belt release and opening the car door. Jamie followed suit, but couldn't undo his belt as his hands were shaking so much. Finally the latch popped free and he jumped out of the car and ran after Elaine, skidding to a halt next to where she was kneeling down.

'It was real,' he said, staring at the things lying in the trail of grey dust streaking the faded black tarmac. He found it difficult to take it all in, but he could see bits of beadworked cloth and leather, part of a shoe and a pile of metal that, as he looked, he saw was the armour the horseman had been wearing.

'I guess, for a moment, it was,' said Elaine, picking up a piece of the cloth. It crumbled in her hand and the light breeze that had picked up took it and blew it away to nothing. She stood up. 'I haven't been drinking, I'm not on any medication – though right now I feel like I ought to be – so what the Sam Hill is going on around here?'

'It's happened again, hasn't it,' said Jamie. It wasn't a question. 'Those people . . . this stuff,' he touched the helmet with his shoe, 'they came from another time.'

'Much as I'd love to tell you to get real,' said Elaine, 'I can't.'

The cross-hairs in the high-powered Leupold Mark 4 scope attached to the H-S Precision take-down .308 hovered, like a delicate hummingbird, over the head of the woman down on the road. He could take both of them out in well under three seconds, no trouble.

'Shall I deep-six them, Mr Dobson?' he muttered into the tiny microphone near his mouth.

'No!' said the terse voice that crackled out of the earpiece of the powerful radio transceiver strapped to his belt. 'Just watch, like I told you . . . watch and wait . . .'

Sprawled on the rock-strewn ground underneath a thorny bush, the man clicked the safety catch on and put the rifle down next to him. Picking up the zoom mini-cam, he continued looking at the scene below him on the road. Then, because that was how he'd been trained, he swung the camcorder slowly from right to left and checked the rest of the area.

'Problem,' he said, pressing the zoom button.

'What?' Dobson's voice hissed back.

'Company . . .'

CHAPTER SEVEN

Timeline: Thursday, 6.05pm

Jamie had just picked up an elaborately decorated spur out of a pile of the grey dust when a shadow fell on his hand. He looked up. Standing some three metres away he saw a figure dressed in boots, jeans and a denim shirt. The sun was now so low in the sky, his face was in shadow.

'Elaine,' he said nervously.

'Yeah?' She didn't stop what she was doing, which was examining the intricate bead design on what looked like a wide leather bracelet.

'There's someone else here.'

Elaine started and dropped the bracelet. 'Where?' she said, looking away down the road.

'Wrong direction,' said the person. His voice sounded younger than he'd imagined it would, thought Jamie. 'Over here.'

Jamie and Elaine both stood up and watched the newcomer walk towards them. As he got closer Jamie could see that he was about eighteen or nineteen years old and had the straight black hair, classic high cheekbones and strong nose of a Native American. Around his neck he was wearing a thin necklace made of bone.

'Who are you . . . how did you get here?' said Elaine.

'You are being watched,' said the boy, stopping by the road where the tarmac began; he spoke very slowly. 'Someone up there,' he nodded his head backwards, 'with a rifle.'

'What!' Elaine looked up at the darkening hills. 'How do you know – are you with the . . . what are they called, Jamie?'

'Special Scientific Office?' said Jamie.

'Yeah, them,' nodded Elaine. 'Or are you one of Mr Dobson's people?'

'Neither.'

'Who are you with then?' demanded Elaine.

'No-one,' said the boy, slipping both thumbs into his jeans pockets and smiling. 'Except maybe the Indian Nation . . .'

'I don't think I can take much more of this weirdness,' sighed Elaine. 'You're telling me there's someone with a gun up there?'

The boy nodded.

'Could be a hunter,' said Jamie.

'Nothing worth shooting round here,' said the boy. 'Except you two.'

'Stop saying that!' Elaine looked nervously up at the hills. 'Why would anyone want to shoot us?'

The boy poked at the pale grey dust with a boot. 'Something's going on, and people are trying to keep it quiet . . . did you feel the shake? Simeon says there's bad magic in the air.'

The man behind the bush watched the three people down on the road. The mini-cam hardly moved, and seemed to have become an extension of his eyes. He lay so still he looked like he could have been carved from rock. And then the scorpion stung him.

He'd been a soldier, a mercenary – in fact a sniper by profession; men in his trade lived by the silence they could keep. When the red-hot needle jabbed into his leg he didn't scream, but he moved like lightning to deal with what had happened to him. It was just unfortunate that he dislodged a small rock with his elbow.

Somewhere up in the gathering dark of the scrub-covered hillside there was a gravelly whisper of small stones on the move, followed by the almost metallic clang of something larger bouncing down the slope towards them. That was it for Elaine.

'Jamie, get in the car – now!' she hissed. 'Tremor or not, we're getting out of here!'

'What about him?' Jamie pointed at the boy. 'We can't leave him.'

'Why not? We don't know who he is – he could be anybody!' Elaine was moving back towards the Honda.

'Elaine . . .' said Jamie. 'Really . . .'

'OK, OK – you want a lift, kid?'

'Uh, yeah . . . that'd be good,' said the boy, as if he had all the time in the world and nothing better to do than give every decision as much thought as it needed.

'Then get your boots in gear and let's go!'

It was only when he was sitting in the car and reaching for his seat-belt that Jamie realized he was still holding the spur he'd picked up from the road. Without thinking, he put it in the bag by his feet and, in his mind's eye, the image of that extraordinary scene flashed up: the young woman, terrified and screaming for her life, and the murderous look on the face of the man on horseback – it was only now that Jamie realized what he was. 'Conquistador . . .' he muttered to himself.

'What's that?' asked Elaine, as she steered the car half off the road so as not to drive over the pile of armour on the tarmac.

'He was a Spanish conquistador . . . that man on the horse,' said Jamie. 'I've seen pictures in a book at school.'

'I've seen those pictures too,' said Elaine, accelerating away down the road. 'But they had their last party in this neck of the woods over four hundred years ago – so what in the name of reason was he doing here now?'

'Bad magic,' said a voice from the back seat of the car.

The big, long-wheelbase Cherokee Chief was parked in a dry riverbed the other side of the hill. Charles Dobson sat in the passenger seat, next to the driver, and behind him a man with large, almost old-fashioned headphones on stared at the glowing screen of a small monitor.

'That shake was pretty low down on the Scale – and it was a dust-out, they touched the sides,' he said. 'Still, at least we know the tech works out here in the real world and not just in the labs.'

The whole of the back of the jeep was filled with a mass of ultra-sensitive electronic equipment, the lights of which flickered and blinked in the gloom. The Cherokee was, in fact, a state-of-the-art mobile seismic detector; its vast array of sensors were able to pick up the tiniest fluctuations in charged air particles that its inventor had discovered preceded movement in the earth's crust. It was unique, one-of-a-kind, but it wasn't being used to give Californians advance warning of earthquakes. The man who'd had paid for it wanted to predict the arrival of other things, like conquistadors.

'Was Parnell *really* going to shoot whatever came through, Dobson?' the man with the headphones asked. 'You know, if it had survived?'

'This is a test run so, yeah, we'd've had to,' Dobson nodded. 'No other way we could've dealt with it right now – but now we know this gizmo works, next time we're gonna try and catch he, she or it . . . if we can.'

'Bad luck those people turning up like that, out of the blue.'

'Which reminds me,' said Dobson, speaking into the tiny headset he was wearing. 'Parnell? Are you there – what's happening?'

A moment's silence followed, and then Parnell's voice came out of a set of speakers under the dashboard, echoing round the interior of the jeep. 'I got stung by some damn scorpion, boss,' he said. 'I knocked a stone and it scared them off.'

'All three of them?'

'Yeah.'

'They take anything?' asked Dobson.

'Can't tell until I get down there,' said Parnell, 'but I don't think so – want me to go and check?'

'Can you walk?'

'I'll survive, it was just a baby,' said Parnell.

'We'll meet you down there,' Dobson nodded at the driver, who started the engine. 'Get the stuff off the road, we'll be with you in a couple of minutes.'

CHAPTER EIGHT

Timeline: Thursday, 6.23pm

Jamie wanted to turn the radio on, do something to break the fragile, spikey silence in the car. Elaine hadn't said a word for ages, and was driving the Honda like she was on some racing circuit (arms straight out, head slightly forward and at well over the speed limit). The guy in the back hadn't said a word since the 'bad magic' comment which had started this whole let's-play-dumb thing off.

He turned in his seat; someone had to get the ball rolling round here, and it looked like he was it. 'My name's Jamie, Jamie Delgado,' he said, putting his hand out.

'Red,' replied the boy, reaching out and shaking Jamie's hand, 'Red Stonegarden . . . nice to meet you.'

'And who the heck's Simeon?' Elaine almost barked. 'What's he know about all this – and why were you out there snooping around?'

'Elaine McFarlane,' Jamie pointed a thumb in her direction, 'she's a reporter with the *Post-Register*.'

'Oh.' Red nodded as if that explained everything.

'So, what gives, Red?' said Elaine. Jamie noticed that, now she was talking again, Elaine had slowed the car down. 'Spill some refried beans.'

'I'm not Mexican, lady.' Red's voice was still calm and slow. 'I'm a full-blood Nez Percés.'

'I don't care if you're Geronimo's grandson,' said Elaine, 'what d'you know about what happened out there?'

'Different tribe . . .'

'Pardon me?' Elaine slowed down even more.

'Geronimo was an Apache,' explained Red, stopping for a moment and then carrying on. 'How much did you see?'

'Everything,' said Jamie quickly. He could tell Elaine was close to losing her temper. 'Right from when the ground shook and the air went all shimmery and the girl ran out into the road.'

'I think you should meet Simeon,' Red nodded to himself in the dark.

'And who . . .'

'He's my uncle,' Red continued, ignoring the interruption. 'What we call a medicine man . . . he knows much more than I do; I was out here for him, keeping a watch.'

'For what?' asked Jamie.

'Open doors,' answered Red.

'OK, I give in,' sighed Elaine. 'Let's go and meet Uncle Simeon – he can't make any less sense than you do, Mr Stonegarden.'

'I wouldn't bet on it,' grinned Red, his even teeth almost glowing in the dashboard light.

While Red gave Elaine directions to his uncle's house,

Jamie phoned home to let his parents know he was OK and would be back even later than he'd expected. They weren't there, and neither was his sister, so he left a garbled message on the answering machine and hoped for the best.

Red had taken them off what passed for the main road in that area and on to a dirt track. The Honda's suspension was having a hard time coping with the potholes and ruts and Elaine was fighting a losing battle to keep the steering-wheel from spinning like a frisbee.

'Is it much further?' she grunted, hauling the wheel over to the right so the car wouldn't hit a large rock in the middle of the road.

' 'Bout half a mile, maybe less,' said Red.

'Do people have cars out here?' asked Elaine.

'Sure, they just don't have tiny little ones with no ground clearance.'

'What happens when it rains?' Elaine brought the car back on to the road. 'And don't say it gets wet.'

'Four-wheel drive . . .' Red's hand snaked out between the seats. 'See those lights up there on the left? That's Simeon's place.'

'I'd be happy as a dog in an old cat's home if I didn't know I'd got to drive back down here to get home,' said Elaine, wincing at the loud scraping noise from right under her feet.

For the last few hundred metres the road almost levelled out and Elaine rolled the car to a halt behind an old Chevrolet truck. Its pale green paintwork was so pitted

48

with rust it looked as if someone had been using it for target practice with a shotgun. Out here, thought Jamie, maybe they had.

'Can that thing actually move?' enquired Elaine.

'Don't judge a book,' said Red. 'It's got a twin-carb V-8 under the hood could pull a tank.'

'The kind of vehicle that driving on these roads really calls for.' Elaine switched off the engine. 'You want to go in first and warn him he's got guests?'

'No, he's cool,' Red tapped Jamie on the shoulder, 'let's do it.'

The night sky was clear, sprinkled with a sugar dust of stars that you never saw living in a city like Los Angeles. Looking up at it took your breath away, and sucking in that clean, almost spicey air made you realize how manufactured urban life was.

'There's millions of them,' said Jamie, quietly.

'Spirits in the sky,' nodded Red.

'Will you two get a move on?' Elaine slammed her door and locked it. 'At some point today I want to get back to reality!'

Red led the way up a narrow concrete path and on to a porch lit by a bare forty-watt bulb, round which circled a doomed squadron of moths. He opened the torn screen door and tapped lightly on the glazed one behind it. 'Simeon?' he said. 'You there?'

'Nowhere else,' replied an older, and if anything, slower version of Red's voice.

'I've got some people to see you – is that OK?'

'My teeth are in, but I'm not biting.'

'I hope this doesn't turn out to be a complete waste of time,' sighed Elaine.

The door opened. 'You can't waste something that's infinite, girl,' said the old man standing in the shadows. 'Time, as I have a feeling you may have found out, is a twisted ribbon . . . want to talk about it?'

Looking past the figure he supposed must be Simeon, Jamie could see the house was dimly lit by a mixture of candles and hurricane lamps, pools of glowing honey surrounded by shadows that seemed to be dancing to some silent, lazy tune. The old man smiled, showing an almost complete set of darkly stained teeth, and waved a hand behind him. The silver rings on each of his fingers glinted.

'Come on in – any friends of Red's . . .' He didn't finish the sentence as he ushered the three of them through the door, shutting it behind them.

Jamie couldn't take his eyes off Simeon. He'd grown up all his life in a city of migrants, where skins of every colour jostled for space – Africans, Mexicans, all types of Europeans, Asians, Chinese, Japanese – but before today he'd never met a real Native American, and Simeon seemed so much more . . . Jamie searched for the right word . . . *authentic* than Red. He had a rolled red and white bandana tied round his head and wore his long grey hair in two plaits that hung down past the pockets of his faded denim shirt. His face was covered in fine lines, almost as if someone had drawn all over it, and he looked as if he'd spent the better part of his long life smiling at a private joke. All he needed to complete the picture was a feather stuck in his headband, thought Jamie.

Red walked ahead into the room, followed by Elaine and Jamie, and as the three of them waited for Simeon to join them a low growl rumbled out of a dark corner.

'Quiet, Fleet,' muttered Simeon, sitting down in an armchair covered in a patterned blanket. 'No call for bad language, boy.'

From out of the gloom a big black dog appeared; he walked over to the armchair, his claws tapping loudly on the wooden floor, and sat down by Simeon. He stared at the newcomers, as if daring them to make a move.

'Don't mind him,' grinned Simeon, 'he's a hot dog with no chilli sauce. Now, Red, how about doing the introductions?'

'Elaine . . . Jamie,' Red pointed at the two of them. 'Simeon,' he nodded at his uncle.

'Pleased to meet you both.'

'Look,' said Elaine, 'if it's not too much trouble, can we get down to business?'

'Always *rushing* about – you people will never understand that going fast often means missing the detail.' Simeon reached over and picked up a small glass, half full of a clear liquid, from a small table in front of him. 'Sit down, Elaine, take it easy, and tell me what you know – or think you know.'

There was a long, low sofa, also covered in blankets, opposite Simeon and everyone sat down – though Jamie found it hard to relax with Fleet's yellow eyes following his every move. There were a few moments silence during which no-one said anything, the only sound being the dog's slow panting, and then Elaine cleared her throat and told Simeon what had happened out on the road.

After she'd stopped talking, Simeon nodded and looked at Jamie. 'That how it went, young-eyes?' he asked.

'Exactly,' said Jamie. 'I couldn't believe what I was seeing!'

'Every time I drive through Beverly Hills I think the same thing.' Simeon shook his head, and then took a sip of his drink. 'When I can't see it, I don't believe in Beverly Hills.'

'I saw what I saw.' Jamie got the impression that, for some reason, the old man thought they were lying – and then he remembered what he had in his bag. 'And I can prove it!'

'You can?' Simeon and Elaine spoke together.

'Sure,' said Jamie, reaching down into the bag on the floor next to him and bringing out the spur he'd picked up. 'Look at this . . .'

He held it in front of him, turning it left and right in his hand; it felt cold and smooth and looked very, very old. Simeon motioned for Jamie to give it to him. Glancing at Elaine and seeing her nod slightly, he handed the spur over.

'Ancient,' whispered Simeon, his eyes closed as he stroked the decorated metal, spinning the sharp wheel. It squeaked – *CHIKK! CHIKK!* – and the sound made

Fleet prick his ears up. 'This was made by old world hands . . . it came across the water and travelled many thousands of miles before it leapt into our time . . .'

'But how on earth did it get here?' said Elaine. 'And what's it got to do with all the other weirdness that's been happening?'

'You know about the other things?' Simeon opened his eyes and put the spur down on the table.

'I know some truly odd things are going on.' Elaine looked at Jamie. 'Young-eyes and I have been checking up on some of them today – we were going home when we witnessed our very own flash of weirdness, and then up popped your nephew with his talk of men with guns and "bad magic".' She nodded at the room. 'Being here kind of rounds off a strange day very nicely.'

'You were lucky Red was out there, could've been trouble.' Simeon shook his head, as if to show how big the trouble could have been. 'You want a coffee or something – maybe one of these?' He held up his glass.

'What is that?' asked Elaine.

'Mescal.'

'I'll have a coffee, black, no sugar,' said Elaine. 'I have to drive back down that dry riverbed you call a road.'

'Jamie?'

'A glass of water'd be great, thanks,' he said.

'Red, hit the kitchen,' said Simeon, 'and bring the bottle when you come back.'

Red got up and wandered off towards the back of the house, switching a light on when he got to the kitchen.

Jamie heard the sound of gas being lit and a kettle being filled.

'You've been good enough to tell me what you know,' said Simeon, taking a final sip and putting his empty glass down on the table next to the spur, 'and now I'll return the compliment.' He sat back in his armchair. 'This would be easier to understand if you were one of us, because people of the tribes are connected with the earth in ways you white folk seem to have lost.'

'I'm very open-minded,' said Elaine. 'Try me.'

'Openness is what it's all about, Elaine.' Simeon's voice had gone kind of dreamy, Jamie thought, and he'd closed his eyes again. 'Just because a door is there doesn't mean it should be opened – bit like that lady Pandora and her box. Some doors are best left closed, locked up and forgotten, because there's no telling what might be behind them.

'We know there's more to this world than the human eye can see, we understand there are forces at work beyond the imaginings of our greatest minds,' Simeon went on, his voice delivering words like the slow drip of a tap. 'This ball of mud we live on is a being, infested with life in much the same way, I have read, that we are host to creatures so small we are unaware of their existence. And it has powers most of us don't have any notion of . . .'

'How does that have anything to do with cowboys in a shopping mall and Spanish conquistadors appearing out of nowhere?' asked Elaine.

'*Some* of us do have a notion of those powers,' continued Simeon, his eyes now open slightly. 'Our medicine men have always been able to tap into them – not control, not even direct, but just try and make contact.'

'Simeon's a medicine man,' said Red, putting a steaming cup of coffee down next to Elaine, and giving a cold glass of water to Jamie. 'He can make the clouds dance.'

'You better believe it,' grinned Simeon.

'I still don't see . . .' said Elaine.

'OK, I'll stop talking like an Indian and give it to you in white man's words – excuse me,' Simeon smiled a wicked smile at Elaine, 'white *woman*'s words. Time ain't no straight line, it's a tangled loop, and where one part of the ribbon touches another, there is a door, so to speak, that can be opened.

'It doesn't happen often, but it happens. We've always known this to be true, and have always left well alone – but I believe someone, somewhere, is making bad magic. This person, I think, is bending the ribbon, which is not good . . . and I also believe it can only get worse.'

'Messing with these kinds of forces, making things happen when they shouldn't, can only lead to trouble,' Simeon continued. 'Push the Earth Spirits, and they push back – and around here that can *really* shake things up!'

'You mean earthquakes?' asked Jamie. 'Maybe the Big One?'

'Posi-*tive*-ly the Big One, young-eyes . . . this stuff carries on the way it's been going and they're gonna be shouting "surf's up!" in Arizona.'

'I believe you've been drinking way too much mescal,' Elaine got up.

'Chance would be a fine thing, with Red forgetting to bring me the bottle!'

'Who could be doing it?' asked Jamie, eager to know more before Elaine dragged him out of the house.

'Hard to say, young-eyes,' replied Simeon as he watched Red go back to the kitchen. 'But I'd bet good money it was no-one in *this* time – even we are losing the skills to talk to the spirits, everything's being drowned out by the frantic babble of the modern world.'

'Well, part of that frantic babble, as you call it, is what pays my wages.' Elaine stood up. 'And I have to get back to my office and add to it – it's been an education meeting you, Simeon . . . even if I don't know quite what it is I've learnt.'

'A pleasure, Elaine . . . call back any time – my door, at least, is always open.'

Jamie picked up the spur and walked round the table to shake Simeon's hand, aware that Fleet had him completely in his sights. 'Thanks,' he said.

'Thank *you*, young-eyes, glad t've met you,' Simeon stood up. 'I'll see you two out with a word of warning – I recommend you be careful, I've got a strong feeling no good's going to come of what's happening out there.'

'Kind of you to worry, Simeon,' said Elaine, 'and you could do yourself a favour – switch to Diet Pepsi and the world *might* begin to appear a little less strange . . .'

CHAPTER NINE

Timeline: Thursday, 8.35pm

Neither of them spoke about what Simeon had said until they were back on the freeway and almost in Mission Hills. What *could* you say? How did you deal with someone who seemed to believe there were doors in time and bad magic was controlling them?

'D'you think he's crazy?' Jamie finally asked, trying not to sound panicky. 'Could he be right about there going to be a major quake because of all this weirdness?'

'Simeon?' said Elaine. 'I don't know, but it sure doesn't make me feel any happier about living here.'

'What if he's right?'

'How *can* he be right?' Elaine indicated and began to overtake a large truck hogging the centre lane. 'There's *got* to be a rational explanation for what's going on!'

'But we saw those two come out of nowhere, Elaine – and then they turned to *dust*!' Jamie had turned in his seat to face Elaine; watching her as she concentrated on her driving, he could see she was as worried as he was. 'And they were from the past – Simeon said that spur was really old and came from Spain.'

'What he *said* was it came from over the water, Jamie,' replied Elaine, 'and that, for all we know, could just as well have meant the LA reservoir back up the road.'

'So where do you think that spur came from then?'

'I don't know,' Elaine flicked a glance at him, 'but I do know someone who might have a better idea . . .'

'Who?'

'The professor who taught me European History at university,' said Elaine. 'I might try calling him after I've dropped you home.'

'*You* went to university and did *history*?' Jamie blurted out.

'What? You think I'm stupid, or something?'

'No . . . no, of course not – it's just, well, you don't seem the type to be doing history,' explained Jamie, 'I always think of guys who do history wearing tweed jackets and smoking pipes.'

'Well *I* wore Tweed perfume and smoked cigarettes.'

'Tweed *perfume*?'

'It's a brand – like Obsession or Poison,' said Elaine, grinning. 'And you're right, I wasn't the type to be doing history . . . I discovered I was a very *now* kind of person, which is why I love newspapers.'

'Not TV?' asked Jamie, glad he didn't seem to have offended Elaine.

'TV is bubblegum, it loses its flavour in a couple of minutes . . . a good newspaper is like a real meal.'

'And the *Post*'s a good newspaper?'

'It's not the *New York Times* or the *Washington Post*,' said Elaine, 'but I don't want to live in either of those places, so it keeps me happy.'

Signs that the Interstate was soon going to split into the Hollywood Freeway and the Golden State appeared up ahead and Elaine moved over to the right to take the Hollywood. She would soon be dropping Jamie off outside his house.

'What are we going to do tomorrow?' he asked.

'Can you get taken to my house tomorrow, instead of the office – say around eight-thirty?' said Elaine.

'I don't suppose my dad'll mind – why?'

'Because I want to carry on looking into more of these "events" and I don't think my esteemed editor is going to be too happy if I disappear out of the office for another whole day on what he will assume is a wild goose chase,' she explained. 'So I simply won't go in.'

It was only when she'd dropped Jamie off and was back on the freeway that Elaine, unable to find her mobile phone, realized Jamie hadn't given it back to her and must still have it – and now she came to think of it, the spur – in his bag. This had been such a strange, mad day her brain was in a whirl and, nagging at the back of her mind, was a little voice that said: *What if Simeon's right? What if the Big One's really coming?*

Pushing aside for now the thought of all the horror and chaos that could bring, and cursing herself for being such a dim-wit, she left the freeway at the next exit, stopped at a big Ralph's supermarket and went in to use the phones.

Elaine stood by the bank of phone booths and frowned at the world. What to do now? She didn't feel like traipsing all the way back to Jamie's, didn't – even though she was tired – feel like going home either and couldn't go to the office in case Henry was there.

What she needed, she suddenly realized, was the kind of rest and relaxation that only old friends could provide. She went back to the phones and made a call. Research, she thought to herself, could take a hike for the evening.

While Elaine was driving down to Santa Monica, Tony Stone was at home, sitting hunched over a table and surrounded by a major untidiness of open books and maps.

Out of curiosity he'd spent his lunch hour at Elaine's desk, looking at the paperwork she'd left behind when she'd gone out with Jamie. He'd found himself having to agree that there was definitely something odd going on – all those incidents *had* to add up to more than just coincidence.

For want of anything better to do, he began reading the news reports and clippings and figured he might have something that needed further investigation. Saying anything too soon might just make him look really foolish – not what a Science Editor should do if he wanted to remain a Science Editor.

Tony left the office early, taking some 'unexplained phenomena' reference material with him, and went home to try and pin down whether he was right or not. Three hours later he still hadn't worked out if he was chasing a red herring or something real, three hours during which he got a blinding headache and began to wish he hadn't given up smoking.

While he waited for a couple of tablets of aspirin to dissolve in a glass of water, Tony wondered what to do next; he felt like he was lost in a maze and he really needed to speak to someone. And the only person who would understand, or care, what he was on about was Elaine. He picked up the phone and dialled her home number, drinking the clear bubbly liquid as he waited for her to answer.

'*This is an answerphone,*' said the tape. '*I'm sorry I'm not home right now, but please leave a message after the tone – or call me on my mobile number if it's urgent . . .*'

When she'd finished reading out her mobile number, and the machine had beeped, Tony left a short message, saying he wanted her to call him as soon as possible, hung up and dialled the mobile. To his great surprise, Jamie's voice answered.

'Are you two still out there?' asked Tony.

'No,' said Jamie. 'My battery was dead and Elaine lent me her phone. I kind of forgot to give it back to her – it was in my camera bag.'

'Do you know where she is?'

'She said she was going to talk to her old history professor, but I don't know where he lives or even his name,' said Jamie.

'What for?' Tony frowned. 'Sudden urge to talk about old times?'

Jamie explained what had happened to them, giving Tony a very condensed version of their day and telling him that Elaine had wanted to find out exactly how old the spur was . . . except she'd forgotten the spur as well.

'Sounds like you guys had quite a time out there,' said Tony.

'Bizarre,' Jamie agreed.

'Look, if Elaine calls you, tell her I need to speak to her urgently.'

'If she doesn't, we're meeting at eight-thirty tomorrow morning, her place,' said Jamie.

'Oh?'

'Yeah, she doesn't want to go into the office in case Henry, Mr Lawrence, doesn't let her back out again.'

'She's probably right,' Tony smiled. 'OK, Jamie, thanks and see you soon.'

Tony put the phone down. He could feel his headache fading at the edges, losing the battle for control of his brain as the Aspirin Cavalry rode to the rescue. Giving silent thanks to the German scientist, whose name he'd forgotten, who'd invented the drug way back in the 1890's (that much he did remember), Tony decided to order some Chinese food. He was so hungry he could eat a horse, especially if it was sweet and sour with a side order of fried rice.

CHAPTER TEN

Timeline: Thursday, 9.45pm

Jamie sat in his bedroom, looking at the spur on the desk in front of him. He didn't know any history professors he could call up at the drop of a hat, but felt he should try and do something rather than just stare at it. And doing something would take his mind off the spooked-out thoughts he was having concerning earthquakes.

'Go look it up' was his father's most favourite over-used phrase – the result of which was that he did have at least two encyclopedias at his disposal, plus another one on CD. And there was always the Net. In this instance, Jamie had to admit, his father was probably right, he should look stuff up. But research required fuel.

His parents were at some neighbours for a barbeque, his sister was in the bathroom doing something disgusting to her hair with what smelled like toxic waste, so he had complete freedom to raid the fridge for whatever took his fancy. Five minutes later Jamie was back up in his room with a jumbo pack of Cool-ranch flavour corn chips, root beer and a plate of assorted edible stuff.

'What next?' he muttered to himself, stuffing a handful of chips in his mouth. He looked over at the serried rank of gold-embossed spines on his bookshelf, thought about getting out the CD version, then glanced at his computer. It was on, right there in front of him. Decision made. Fast facts, unlike fast food, were not bad for you. But the trouble with random access was that you could spend hours jumping about, reading captions, watching movie clips and generally grazing in the fact farm without actually *getting* anywhere. Which is exactly what Jamie did, for a while.

Finally realizing he was wasting time, he looked up 'conquistador', scoped the articles and pictures and found he was none the wiser when it came to the subject of spurs. So he keyed in 'spur' and there, amongst a screen of pictures, he saw an example labelled *Spanish, 16th century* that looked sort of similar to the one on the desk right next to him.

'So far, so what,' he muttered, and then wondered what to do next. What he *really* needed was to get someone to look at his spur, but how? He sat and ate chips for a couple of minutes, finishing off the root beer and suddenly sat up. 'Teejay!' he yelped, grabbing the phone.

Thomas Jefferson Morgan III, a.k.a. Teejay, was the class net-jockey and general computer whiz-kid; the kind of guy who seemed to spend every minute he could hunched over a keyboard. Described like that he sounded a total disaster area, friend-wise, but somehow he managed to be hip *and* clever at the same time. No mean feat.

Teejay answered the phone on its second ring. 'Morgan's Magic Mainframe,' he said. 'Friend or fax?'

'Teejay, it's Jamie . . . I've got a problem I think you

might be able to solve.'

T.J. Morgan II, Teejay's father, was something big in oil and made MONEY. Teejay's room in the vast Spanish-style hacienda mansion was like a computer hardware showroom. He had everything, including a couple of wide-screen Macs, three linked PCs, a laser printer, a couple of inkjets and some extra-special cable hook-up that sounded impressive, although Jamie had no real idea what it did. Teejay was connected.

'Where'd you get this?' he asked, turning the spur over in his hands.

'Found it out in the desert, kind of,' said Jamie, the sweat from his bike ride over to Teejay's house cooling uncomfortably fast in his air-conditioned room.

'Nice piece . . . what d'you need me for, history's not really my bag.'

'Put it on the Net for me,' said Jamie, 'so some guy whose bag *is* history can tell me where it comes from.'

'Can do.' Teejay put his hand out. 'Gimme . . .'

Clearing a space on a nearby desk, Teejay put the spur on a sheet of white paper, moved a lamp so it that it was lit properly and fired off a couple of shots with a digital camera he'd pulled out of a drawer. Jamie just sat and watched, beyond impressed that a hi-res picture of the spur was Net-ready in less time than it would take him to make a decent sandwich.

'And now?' he asked.

'And now I search out a likely site and post the image.

And then we wait to see if anyone takes the time to send us an answer.'

While Teejay set about finding the right kind of place to send the image, Jamie wandered round his room, idly looking at stuff. Which was how he came to find himself in front of a map of California pinned to the wall; he stared at the dark spine of the San Andreas Mountains and remembered what Simeon had said earlier in the day.

'You got anything on earthquakes, Teej?'

'Feel free to use one of the other machines, dude,' Teejay waved vaguely behind him. 'You'll find something out there.'

Jamie smiled. 'Go look it up, right?'

'Won't know till you do, dude…'

Jamie found screeds of stuff 'out there'. Time flew by as he read articles about the geography of California, downloaded highly technical maps of the state and read up on the history of the San Andreas Fault. The next thing he knew it was more than an hour later and Teejay was calling him over to the screen he was sitting at.

'We have an answer,' he said.

'Already?'

'A lucky break, some guy in San Diego who's on-line collects this stuff.' Teejay pointed to the laser printer next to him. 'I'm printing out now.'

As a piece of A4 paper slid out of the printer Jamie picked it up and turned it over. 'It says *"Appears to be* conquistador's spur,"' he read. '"Early 1500's, possibly made in Toledo, Spain. Do you have the pair? Do you want to sell?"'

'The stuff you can do in cyberspace!' grinned Teejay. 'Don't you just love it?'

'You're a hero, Teej, I owe you one,' Jamie looked at his watch. Eleven forty-five. 'I'd better slide off, I've got an early start tomorrow.'

'D'you want to answer this guy?' asked Teejay. 'Like, yes or no on the sale question?'

'Not mine to sell,' replied Jamie. 'Look, can I take the stuff I got off that web site?'

'Sure,' Teejay looked at Jamie. 'Are you up to something, you got a scam going?'

'No . . . no scam,' said Jamie, suddenly embarrassed. 'It's something to do with a story the reporter I'm working with on the paper – you know, my holiday job? – something she's doing.'

'Kay, that's cool, client confidentiality and all that stuff,' Teejay smiled. 'I understand . . . just let me in on the scoop when you can, right?'

'Sure, Teej, and thanks again.'

'No sweat.'

Actually he worked up a lot more sweat as he rode back home. After a quick shower (the bathroom still smelt like a bad day at the chemical plant) he went back to his room and was about to collapse into bed when he saw the papers he had brought back with him. He picked up one of the maps, the one showing the plate formations running through California, and went and got his atlas. Something had just occurred to him.

He looked at where the towns were that they'd visited that day, and checked the whereabouts of a few of the other places he could remember from Elaine's notes that things had happened at. Then he looked at the print-out again. A shiver ran down his back, like a drop of cold water. What had Simeon said? *Push the Earth Spirits and they push back?* It looked very much like they were pushing all the way along the San Andreas Fault . . .

Charles Dobson put the phone down and smiled; it was late, he was tired, but that was all right. Things were going smoothly. His network of contacts had come up with the name of the woman who had turned up while they were monitoring the 'hot' site – the one the over-enthusiastic Parnell had wanted to rub out.

He looked at the notes he'd made during his phone conversation; the woman, Elaine McFarlane, was a reporter and it looked like she'd taken something from the roadside. One of the spurs was missing. This needed checking out . . . in fact, as he had McFarlane's address, he'd get the process under way right now.

Dobson picked up the phone again and dialled a number. 'Parnell,' he said. 'I've got a job for you . . .'

Tony was sound asleep in front of the TV when the phone went. He always kept the ringer down low because he hated the noise it made, so he missed the call; it was from Elaine. She'd checked her answering machine for messages and was returning his call.

Waking at midnight, and feeling like something the cat had dragged in, he stumbled into bed without realizing the phone had gone. It wasn't till he woke up at six thirty the next morning that he discovered her message.

Seeing the flashing red light, he hit the rewind button and listened as Elaine's voice came out of the tinny speaker:

'Tony, got your message,' she said, *'but it's eleven o'clock and I'm beat . . . I've had one too many glasses of wine and I'm staying with a friend in Santa Monica. Jamie's got my mobile, but I'm meeting him at my place at eight-thirty tomorrow morning; why not swing by and we'll get some breakfast and talk then . . . good night, and sweet dreams.'*

The machine clicked off and Tony glanced at his watch; there was enough time for him to have a shower and shave before he had to leave to meet Elaine and Jamie. Grabbing a small radio he headed for the bathroom.

Chapter Eleven

Timeline: Friday, 7.55am

Jamie's father had wanted to get to his office earlier than usual and he'd asked if Elaine would mind him being dropped at her house just before eight. Jamie had meant to call her and check, but had run out of time, and had been in such a rush to get out of the house he'd only just managed to grab a buttered muffin and his bag. In it, along with his camera, were his fully charged phone (and charger, just in case), Elaine's phone, the spur and the print outs. Running down the drive to join his dad, he was sure turning up early wouldn't be a problem.

By the time Jamie realized Elaine wasn't home, his father's car was a dot at the end of the street. He'd rung the bell and knocked on the window, but the door had carried on staring blankly back at him; it was no use looking for a phone – her mobile was in his bag – so he'd just have to wait and wonder.

He was beginning to think she'd forgotten that he was coming over and had gone to work without him when a car pulled up opposite the bungalow, the driver waving at him. Jamie couldn't work out who it was – he didn't recognize the car and didn't know anyone in the area – but then he saw Tony Stone getting out.

'What are you doing here, Tony?' he called across the street.

'Meeting you guys for breakfast – isn't she back yet?'

'Back from where?'

'She stayed the night down with a friend in Santa Monica,' said Tony, coming up the pathway. 'She called last night and said to meet here at eight-thirty . . . not like her to be late.'

'Probably overslept,' said Jamie, looking left and right past Tony, checking the street. 'Or maybe some screw-up on the freeway – my dad was listening to some classical station in the car that doesn't do traffic reports, did you hear anything?'

'I was tuned to the same station,' shrugged Tony. 'Whatever, we'll wait out here.'

Jamie was about to ask why Elaine had got him to come over when he thought he heard something inside the house, like a door closing or a floorboard creaking. He looked round, frowning. 'Did you hear that?' he asked.

'What?'

'That noise.'

'I must be getting old, I didn't hear a thing.' Tony walked over to one of the windows and put both hands up and peered through the glass. 'Can't see anything, either.'

'Has Elaine got a cat?' asked Jamie.

'Dunno,' said Tony. 'Let's check the back, shall we?'

Jamie followed him round the side of the one-storey house and down the narrow passageway to the rear. It was cool and shaded as the thick, bushy hedge separating Elaine's property from the one next door had grown up and over, creating a kind of green tunnel.

The back yard was as untidy as her desk at the *Post*; the grass hadn't been cut for ages, the flowerbeds were a riot of admittedly colourful weeds and in one corner stood a sad, rusty barbecue that looked like it had become an old spiders' home.

'She's not one of the world's great gardeners,' commented Tony, walking round an old aluminium sunbed whose faded plastic webbing had definitely seen better days. He stopped by the back door and pointed at the plastic flap set in the bottom panel. 'She's got a cat . . . or at least she had one at some time . . .'

Jamie was a few metres behind Tony, looking in through the large glass patio doors at what he thought must be Elaine's lounge, when he saw it. A shadow moving across the open doorway at the back of the room – not a cat, but a person. For a moment he didn't know what to do. It happened so quickly, but he was sure he'd seen it. 'There's someone in there, Tony,' he said quietly, 'someone's in the house . . . what do we do now?'

'Are you sure?' said Tony, coming back to look.

'I saw someone's shadow – should we call the cops?' whispered Jamie, kneeling down and unzipping his camera bag. 'I've got Elaine's phone and it's still got a charge – I checked this morning.'

'We should get back out to the front,' said Tony, disappearing down the passageway.

Closing his bag, Jamie was about to get up and go after him when he heard footsteps. And then he felt something cold and metallic on his neck.

'Get up,' said a hushed voice. 'You're coming with me.'

Jamie froze, unable to move.

'I said get *up!*'

Bag in hand, Jamie did as he was told. An arm roughly gripped him round his neck and he found himself being frogmarched into Elaine's kitchen; through it he could see the shadowy figure of a man by the front door and from somewhere down the street he heard the sound of tyres laying a significant amount of their rubber on the tarmac and an engine almost howling in pain.

'I got a hostage,' he heard the man holding him say.

The person at the door whirled round, snarling. 'You *idiot*, Bascombe – the last thing we need's a hostage!' he hissed. 'Get rid of him and let's get outta here!'

Jamie heard a loud dull click . . . and somewhere in his head a small frightened voice told him it was the hammer of the gun being pulled back. *Get rid of him*, the man had just said. He was going to die.

'Put the damn gun away, Bascombe!'

Jamie saw the man open the front door, bright light streaming into the house and then things began to happen so fast he would later be unable to remember exactly what went on. He was suddenly thrown to one side and found himself staggering into a couple of stools as the man, Bascombe, ran past him and out of the house after his accomplice.

Picking himself up, his legs feeling oddly weak, he

couldn't figure out what to do next; what he wanted was to find Tony and Tony was out front, so without thinking he ran for the open door.

Skidding to a halt on the step he saw the two men running at full pelt, Bascombe with his gun still in his hand. He saw Tony moving towards them across the lawn, heard a sharp – *K-RAKK!* – realized Bascombe had fired and saw Tony fall over. Shocked, he watched the two men carry on running towards the street; saw a black van screech to a halt, rocking backwards and forwards on its suspension as its side door was flung open; saw the two men hurl themselves in as the van started accelerating away down the road, its rear end fishtailing like mad.

There was another squeal of brakes and a loud blast of a horn as the van swerved to avoid a head-on collision with a car coming down the road. The black van mounted the pavement, ploughed a wide trench in the grass verge which sent great clods of earth flying up behind it, bounced back on to the road and screamed off.

And then, silence.

The car that had so nearly had its bonnet restructured still sat in the road, its driver's door slowly opening. It took a moment for Jamie to realize it was a Honda, that it was in fact Elaine getting out of it.

Jamie, his heart pounding, mouth dry, remembered Tony – he'd been shot! Turning, he saw Tony was getting up off the ground. 'Are you OK?' Jamie yelled, strumbling towards him.

'Apart from maybe needing to change my trousers,

fine . . .'

'You didn't . . . ?'

'No,' grinned Tony. 'I just got grass stains all over them.'

'What the hell's going on?' shouted Elaine as she ran over to them.

'You've had visitors,' said Tony, 'and we disturbed them – has this got anything to do with the story, Elaine?'

'How should I know?' She shook her head. 'I'd better get the car out of the middle of the road – wait for me.'

'Should we call the police now?' Jamie called after her.

'No,' she called back, 'I want to see what they've done first.'

'*What* happened?' Dobson almost crushed the handset in his fist he was so angry.

'Kinda outstayed our welcome,' replied Parnell. He was standing outside the van, which was parked round the back of an empty shop having its numberplates changed. 'And then the boy and another guy turned up.'

'This was supposed to be an in-and-out job,' said Dobson. 'Why were you still there?'

'Couldn't find the spur *any*where, almost took the place apart.' Parnell made a swift circular motion with his left hand as he spoke, urging the man working on the van to hurry it up.

'What about a computer – did she have one?'

'Yeah, but Bascombe took for ever to crack her password,' said Parnell. 'And when he did he said she had more files on that thing than you'd find at a convention of manicurists.'

'Why didn't you get out sooner?'

'Lotta work putting things back the way they were, boss – she wasn't supposed to've known we'd been there, is what you said.' Parnell gave the thumbs-up to the man who was showing the new plate, and nodded for him to get back in the van.

'So what was Bascombe doing taking hostages and shooting at them?' Dobson enquired sarcastically.

'He can tell you himself, when he comes round, boss,' said Parnell. 'I kind of lost my temper with him.'

'I don't blame you.' Dobson looked out of his office window, fifteen storeys up in a Century City tower. 'Go back to the warehouse, I'll meet you there in an hour.'

'Check.'

'Oh, and Parnell?'

'Boss?'

'Call Tirrel and get him over to McFarlane's place *now*,' said Dobson. 'I want a tag on her car first chance he gets, OK?'

Dobson cut the connection and put the phone down. The last thing he wanted was some nosy reporter sniffing around.

He looked at his watch; nearly eight-thirty. He'd clear up a few things and then he'd go to meet Parnell at the warehouse and sort out Bascombe. But first he had to make his daily call to Mr Whelan.

As with most men with more money than they knew what to do with, Cletus Whelan expected to be able to get what he wanted exactly when he wanted it. He did not like to be told there were problems with anything. 'I pay *you* so *I* don't have problems, Dobson!' was one of Mr Whelan's favourite phrases, and Charles Dobson hated it. He sometimes thought about quitting his job, but then he thought about how much Whelan was paying him so that he didn't have problems, and knew that he couldn't quit. He didn't so much get a salary as win the lottery every month.

Sighing, mainly because at the moment he didn't have any time to spend any of his money, he dialled the phone number only two other people in the whole world knew about and waited for it to be answered . . .

Chapter Twelve

Timeline: Friday, 9.20am

Elaine had called the police as soon as she found out a shot had been fired. There was nothing much any of them could tell the two uniforms who'd turned up fifteen minutes later in their black-and-white, siren blasting and lights flashing. None of them had taken the licence number of the black van, and neither Jamie nor Tony had really got anything but the briefest look at the men who had run out of the house.

A swift check had shown that there was no sign of a break-in, and the cops had noted how tidily the place had been searched. It was, in their considered opinion, a very professional piece of work, and they almost made it sound like Elaine should be glad the two men had been so good at their job.

'Trying to take a hostage and firing a gun at an unarmed man was a pretty dumb move,' commented Elaine, as the policemen were going out the door.

'Burglars, especially the career types, hate being caught on the premises, ma'am,' said one of the cops. 'The one who grabbed your young friend,' he nodded at Jamie, 'was obviously the panicky type.'

'Obviously,' said Elaine. 'Are you going to look for the bullet?'

'Not much point, ma'am,' the cop jerked his thumb the way the gun had been fired. 'It could be anywhere, all we can be thankful for is that it didn't hit anyone.'

'A-men to that,' said the other cop.

'Urban cowboys,' said Elaine, watching the two men walk back to their car, half a hardware shop hanging off their belts.

Once Elaine had made sure Jamie was all right she checked the bungalow again, just to satisfy herself that nothing really had been taken, locked up and they went to a nearby diner for a late breakfast. It was only after they'd eaten, and Jamie had calmed down by telling them what had happened to him another couple of times, Elaine sat back, pushed her plate away and waved to the waitress for more coffee.

'So, Tony,' she said, 'why'd you call last night?'

Tony picked his briefcase off the floor. 'It's to do with that story you're looking into, the one about all the strange stuff going on.'

'What about it?'

'I did some work on it last night . . .'

'What kind of work?' interrupted Elaine.

'Don't be so suspicious – the helpful kind, not the I'm-trying-to-steal-your-thunder kind,' smiled Tony. 'I just spent a bit of time last evening looking at your notes, more in the hope that you were chasing a mirage than anything else, and by the time I'd finished I couldn't see the wood for the trees . . .' He took his notes out of his briefcase and laid them on the table top. 'I have no idea what all this means.'

Elaine leaned back. 'Join the club, Tony,' she said.

'I've got an idea,' said Jamie, reaching back into his bag. He took out the map he'd downloaded from the net at Teejay's and placed it on the table. 'All these weird incidents make a line that follows the San Andreas Fault, all six hundred miles of it,' he said. 'Scarey, huh?'

'How'd you find that out?' exclaimed Elaine, staring at Jamie in amazement.

Jamie sat back and told them what he'd done the night before, how he and Teejay – well, to be honest, he said, mostly Teejay – had got a confirmation that the spur was really old and from Spain, just like Simeon had said.

'And while he was doing that,' he went on, 'I did some research of my own into earthquakes, and I realized what was happening . . . freaked me out.'

Tony and Elaine didn't say anything for a long time, and then Tony asked who the heck Simeon was.

'The guy I told you about on the phone,' said Jamie, and Tony nodded.

'We ended up out in the boonies,' said Elaine, 'getting a lecture on messing with the Earth Spirits from a Nez Percés medicine man.'

'And what did he have to say for himself?' asked Tony.

'He said there was bad magic going on,' said Jamie, 'and things might get shaken up.'

'How right he could be.' Tony started picking the papers up off the table and looked closely at them.

'Were you here in '94, Elaine?' Elaine nodded. 'Well if *that* was anything to go by, the real thing will be a *total* nightmare.'

'I wasn't even born,' Jamie finished his juice, 'but my dad said it was pretty intense.'

'We were all just lucky it happened so early . . .' Tony shook his head at the memory, then re-focussed. 'And you want to know what's really weird? I just saw some figures yesterday, in one of the e-newsletters I get, and they showed a dangerous build-up in plate activity in recent weeks . . .'

'I think,' said Elaine at last, 'we should pay another visit to Mr Medicine Man.'

'Why's that?' said Tony.

'Much as I'm loathe to admit it, he seems to know more about this than anyone else,' Elaine looked over and caught the waitress's eye, 'and I need to find out everything I can.'

'I was beginning to think this was a dead-end story,' said Tony. 'Just a lot of coincidences and nothing more – maybe it's time I did some more checking, got some info from various places about recent activity along the line.'

'Go for it,' said Elaine. 'We can't know too much about this – if we want to convince anyone else the Big One's coming we're going to have to have more than just a few dots on a map and the say-so of someone as wacky as Simeon.'

'What shall I tell Henry?' asked Tony.

'That you've no idea where I am – which, as I shan't tell you where I'm going, will be the absolute truth.'

Elaine paid the bill, and the three of them got up and filed out of the diner. They walked slowly over to where their cars were parked, Jamie trailing slightly behind as Tony and Elaine talked some business.

'Keep in touch,' said Tony as he unlocked his car, 'and be careful – that break-in at your place wasn't just some kids after a bit of extra cash, whoever it was was looking for something specific; they had guns, they had back-up and they know who you are and where you live. You're a big girl, and you can look after yourself, but look what nearly happened to Jamie . . .'

'We'll be fine, Tony,' she said. 'The worst thing that could happen to us where we're going is we get a flat tyre driving up Simeon's lame excuse for a road.'

'Don't underestimate things.' Tony opened the car door and flung his briefcase over on to the passenger seat. 'I think you've trodden on someone's toes without knowing you've done it . . . someone big.'

Elaine and Jamie watched Tony drive out of the parking lot and into the morning traffic.

'Prophet of doom,' she said, taking her car keys out of her jacket pocket.

'You don't think we should be careful?'

'Of course we should . . . but if I worried about stepping on people's toes all the time I'd never get my job done,' Elaine looked over at Jamie. 'You still want to come?'

'No question!'

'Let's hit the road then.'

Neither of them noticed the man not really reading his newspaper in a car across the street. On the seat next to him a small black box began to beep.

The warehouse Dobson had rented some six months ago was in Downtown, a couple of blocks off Olympic Boulevard. It was an anonymous building you wouldn't give a second glance to as you drove by, which was just how he liked it, and the sign outside said it belonged to something called the Direct Corp., a dummy company he'd set up to buy the lease.

Pulling up outside he sounded the horn quickly twice, waited a couple of seconds, and then did one long beep. It was the signal for the doors to be opened so he could drive in off the street. He lowered the window, heard the whine of an electric motor starting and watched as the wide metal door began to move slowly upwards. Inside he could see a shadowy figure looking out at him. Parnell, thought Dobson, checking that it's me. He nodded to himself; he was a good man, reliable, if a little hasty sometimes. Dobson saw Parnell waving for him to drive in and he took his foot off the brake.

The door was closing by the time Dobson had parked and Parnell was waiting to go with him up to the office. 'Bascombe's upstairs,' he said. 'Want to go talk to him?'

'There's not a lot to say, except he's off the active list until further notice and I'm sending him back to New

Mexico,' said Dobson, thinking that, no matter how much money you had at your disposal, it could never completely guarantee the quality of what you bought. Especially when it came to staff. 'I can't afford to have a loose cannon blundering about, not when things are coming to a head.'

'He's been A1 reliable up till now,' Parnell shrugged, 'but you're right, boss, he blew it when things got intense . . . he's not a bad guy, though, so don't be too hard on him.'

'You've already done that.'

'Heat of the moment.' Parnell stopped and let Dobson go up the metal stairs first. 'What are we going to do about the girl?'

'She's a reporter, works for the *Post-Register*,' said Dobson. 'We know who she is, where she works, we've got her car tagged and I'm getting more deep background on her.'

'And the other two?'

'The older guy's the Science Editor on the paper.' Dobson stopped, one hand on the handle of the door at the top of the stairs. 'Collins ran a trace on his car and the car that dropped the kid off . . . some business type turns out is a friend of the paper's owner.'

'They a team, or something?' asked Parnell. 'He was with her yesterday.'

'Who knows,' said Dobson, turning the handle. 'Whatever they're up to, we can deal with it . . .'

Chapter Thirteen

Timeline: Friday, 12.15pm

The sun had reached its zenith and the temperature was well into the eighties. Not summer, but hot nonetheless. They were back on the freeway and crawling out of LA, on their way back to Simeon's house. Jamie had suggested phoning to make sure someone was there – it was, after all, a long way to go to find an empty house – but Elaine didn't have his number. In fact she didn't know Simeon's surname, or a proper address, to be able to ask the phone company to find if he even *had* a number. It was entirely possible, she'd said, that someone like him wouldn't have one, as staggering a concept as that might be, in the 21st century.

After taking a couple of wrong turns, mainly because it had been dark when they'd been driving home and nothing looks the same in the daylight, they finally found the road leading to Simeon's house.

'Hasn't gotten any better overnight,' said Elaine, as the Honda bounced in and out of the cavernous potholes.

'The truck's still there,' said Jamie.

'Let's hope he hasn't gone for a walk,'

'In *this* heat?'

'I got the distinct impression his brains are fried already,' smiled Elaine. 'A little more sun wouldn't make a lick of difference to that old guy!'

'So why've we come back?' asked Jamie.

'Because, mad though I suspect he may be, I think he knows things we don't about what's been going on.'

The car rolled to halt behind the old Chevy and Elaine was hauling on the hand-brake when Jamie saw the screen door open; Red stepped out on to the porch and waved. 'Almost like we were expected,' he said, half jokingly.

'Somehow, just *knew* you'd be back,' nodded Simeon as he came out of the kitchen. 'Want a drink?' he asked, showing Elaine the can of Diet Pepsi he had in his hand.

'Somehow I didn't think you'd take my advice,' she replied.

'You're never too old to take advice.'

'Or too experienced to ask for help,' said Elaine. 'Mind if we sit down?'

'Best way to have a pow-wow.' Simeon prodded Fleet and shooed the sleeping black dog off his chair. 'Like I need it keeping warm in this weather . . .'

'I've got some stuff to show you, charts and things Jamie here put together.' Elaine took the papers out of her bag and spread out the map. 'Know what this is?'

'What you folks call the San Andreas Fault,' said Simeon. 'We never had a name for it, but we've always known it was there – has a way of reminding you every so often, too.'

'Right.' Elaine then put the map with the red dots down next to it. 'This mean anything?'

Simeon leaned forward, squinting, and Red stood up to have a closer look as well. 'I got it figured,' he said, slowly tapping a couple of places on the map. 'It's where there've been breakthroughs, Uncle.'

'Correct-imento, nephew!' Simeon sat back and took a pull on his can. 'Welcome to Weird City, sister – I'm gonna be interested to see how you write *this* particular story up.'

Simeon, thought Jamie, had to be one of the strangest people he'd ever met – a jazzy, jive-talking, grizzled old medicine man.

'I can't write it up until I know what's going on,' said Elaine.

'And?'

'And I wondered if you'd like to tell me . . . as you two seem to know more than anyone else about it.'

'Want a drink?' asked Simeon.

'Could kill for one,' said Elaine, Jamie nodding in agreement.

'No need to do that,' Simeon glanced at Red, who got up and went to the kitchen. 'So, what do you want to know?'

'Everything,' said Elaine.

Simeon burst out laughing, his old, lined face cracking like earth in a drought, and he sat back in his chair shaking his head. Jamie looked at Elaine, wondering if Simeon really was as crazy as she thought.

'You OK, Uncle?' asked Red, coming back with a six-pack of cans. 'What's so funny?'

'Yesterday she thought I was madder'n a stuck pig,' cackled Simeon, nodding at Elaine, 'and, not even twenty-four hours later, she's back wanting to know more!' He suddenly stopped laughing and looked directly at Elaine. 'Something happen last night?'

'This morning,' said Elaine. 'My house got burgled.'

'Goes with the territory, where you live . . . so I hear.'

'This wasn't an ordinary break-in,' explained Elaine, 'they didn't steal anything . . . they were looking for something, and I don't know what it was, or whether they found it.'

'They had guns, and there was a whole gang of them,' added Jamie. 'I nearly got kidnapped and we got shot at.'

'Sorry to hear that,' said Simeon. 'I did warn you to be careful.'

'I apologize if I was a tad big-headed yesterday.' Elaine popped a can and took a long pull on it. 'Sometimes you forget your manners in this business.'

'No apology necessary . . . I don't blame you for being sceptical, for not believing a word I said,' Simeon dug a hand into one of his shirt pockets and brought out a small carved wooden figure. 'When I was a boy, younger than young-eyes here, people believed things like this could protect them against evil – and some still do – but nowadays, in this *modern* world, we know better, don't we, Red?'

'Maybe,' Red smiled a slow smile.

'Maybe is right,' Simeon went on. 'The thing of it is, we generally hate to admit we don't know things, don't understand what's happening. There always has to be an answer that fits the facts – an answer that makes sense.'

'And sometimes the answer *doesn't* make sense, is that what you're saying?'

'On the button, my dear.'

'Well, I'm here to tell you that I've left all my late-twentieth-century prejudices behind, Simeon . . . today we're here to listen.'

'I told you all yesterday I thought someone was pushing the Earth Spirits, and I didn't think it was anyone in this time.' Elaine nodded. 'Well, I don't think, I *know*.'

'How?'

'If you believe what I'm telling you, you don't need to know the *how* of it – that's the way believing works, Elaine.'

'You can get sold all kinds of rubbish if you believe *every*thing you're told,' said Jamie. 'People used to think the Earth was flat *and* the centre of the universe, till someone proved them wrong.'

'That Copernicus was quite a guy,' said Simeon. 'But he proved his point, showed them *he* was right and *they* were wrong.'

'And you can prove what you're saying?' asked Jamie.

'Sure can.'

Jamie was about to say 'How?', but stopped himself just in time and waited, eyebrows raised and a questioning look on his face.

'You a cool kid, young-eyes,' grinned Simeon. 'Not gonna catch Jamie out in a hurry, am I!'

'So what's the proof, Simeon?' said Elaine.

The old man looked at her. 'I know where there's a door,' he said, 'an open door back to where *I* believe the cause of all this trouble is . . .'

Charles Dobson sat alone in the small office in the old Downtown warehouse. It was quiet, and he used the time to think about what his next move should be; he'd torn a strip off Bascombe, had Parnell take him directly to the airport and put him on the first flight to New Mexico – now he had to figure out what to do with the McFarlane woman.

He knew, deep down, what should be done and he knew exactly how to do it. He started to work out how to explain it to Parnell, and then realized it would be so much quicker, so much *easier*, if he did it himself.

It had been a long time since he was out on the road; his days as an Agency operative had left him with a few scars and a load of memories. But he had been good, and, like riding a bike, he'd no doubt it would all come back to him once he got out there again. Strangely, the thought of getting his hands dirty once more made him feel excited, and he realized how much he missed actually *doing* things, as opposed to telling other people what to do and losing his temper when they got it wrong.

Reaching across the metal desk he picked up the phone and dialled a number, waiting for it to be picked up.

'Parnell,' said a voice.

'When you've finished, meet me back here,' said Dobson. 'There's something I want to set up.'

CHAPTER FOURTEEN

Timeline: Friday, 3.00pm

'So, there's an open door,' said Elaine. 'What does that mean?'

'It means someone can go back and try to stop the man I think is doing this from wrecking our present and his future,' explained Simeon.

'Who?' asked Elaine.

'Who what?'

'Who's going to go back?'

'I am,' said Red, looking a little embarrassed as everyone turned to stare at him.

'No-one round here takes a blind bit of notice of me any more, 'cept Red,' shrugged Simeon. 'They're all too interested in their satellite dishes and mobile phones to want to listen to an old man who doesn't even *have* a phone.'

Jamie looked at Elaine, wondering if she remembered their conversation in the car. He found it difficult to imagine what life would be like living in a house where you couldn't call up a friend whenever you wanted.

'My knowledge isn't important to them,' Simeon went on. 'It's not relevant – *I'm* not relevant any more.'

'They've lost the way, Uncle,'

'True, boy,' sighed Simeon, 'but I think you and I are the only thing left between us and a big bit of hell on earth if we don't stop these things happening – and soon.'

'When's he going?' asked Elaine.

'Today,' said Simeon. 'We haven't got much time left. Things are coming to a head.'

'I want to go as well,' Elaine sounded very firm.

'Me too,' chipped in Jamie quickly – the idea of going back in time, just walking from one era to another, was exciting, fascinating and not a little bit scary. But he didn't want to be left out.

'Hold up a sweet minute!' Simeon waved both hands at them and shook his head. 'This ain't some day-trip to Universal City to go on the *Back to the Future* ride! It's gonna be dangerous – heck I don't *really* want to send Red, but I've got no choice, I'm too old to go gallivanting around any more . . .'

'Things aren't too cosy for me right here, right now,' said Elaine, 'and, even though I am a mere woman, I *can* take care of myself, Simeon.'

'But what about young-eyes?'

'I can take care of myself too!' Jamie frowned. 'I may be still at school, but I'm not a *kid*!'

'I don't know . . .' said Elaine.

'You can leave him here with me,' suggested Simeon, 'collect him on the way back – *if* you come back . . .'

Elaine was silent for some time; the only sounds in the house seemed to be Fleet's loud breathing, coming from behind the sofa where he'd gone back to sleep, and the screen door lazily slamming in the breeze. Finally she looked at Jamie and then at Simeon. 'Sounds weird I know, but after what happened today it just *may* be safer for Jamie to come with me.'

'Yes!' Jamie yelled, delighted.

'This some kind of female logic?' asked Simeon.

'No, just logical,' said Elaine. 'It occurred to me that whoever's after what they *think* I know must have serious resources behind them. And if that's true they may be able to find out where I've been and come looking.'

'Send him back home, then.'

'They sure as heck must know where *that* is by now, Simeon!'

'If you say so, girl, if you say so.' Simeon got up. 'If you're all going, we better get a move on, get you kitted up for the journey – they don't have hamburger joints and motels where you guys are headed.'

They spent the next hour putting together three sets of the oddest survival gear Jamie had ever seen. For a start, Simeon made Elaine and Jamie change their clothes – it wouldn't do, he said, to turn up wearing Timberlands, Swatch watches and Calvin Klein jeans. Searching through cupboards and chests of drawers, he assembled enough relatively clean stuff for each of them, including thick blanket jackets and an old pair of leather boots each, which Jamie found just about fitted if he wore two pairs of socks. This, he thought to himself, wasn't going to be anything like Scout camp.

Everything else they were to take with them was rolled up in three old blankets and secured with cracked leather straps; what went in each one was some dried strips of meat, a full water flask, a knife, a tinderbox – for lighting fires – and a spare set of clothes. Once everything was ready Simeon sat down.

'Red, here,' he cocked a thumb at his nephew, 'he's named after Red Echo, one of the bravest Nez Percés chiefs there ever was, and I taught him as much as it's possible for a twentieth-century boy to know about where you're off to. So what he says goes, that has to be understood.'

Elaine nodded and Jamie looked at Red, wondering what it must be like to have a foot in two cultures like he did.

'You are going to have the privilege of seeing where I come from,' Simeon went on, 'and it won't be *nothing* like the movies, not even *Dances With Wolves* – I'm just warning you so's you won't be too surprised. And, most important of all, you mustn't take anything with you from this time, no torches or calculators, no modern gizmos . . .'

'What about the stuff you've given us?' enquired Jamie.

'That's all real old, young-eyes,' said Simeon. 'Won't cause any problems.'

'We should move soon,' said Red. 'I want to get some miles behind us before nightfall.'

'Ain't you forgetting something, nephew?' Red frowned. 'The ceremony,' said Simeon. 'We have to do the ceremony . . .'

It was hot and airless. All the blinds in the house were drawn and, even though it was still light outside, candles had been lit. Simeon had disappeared, leaving Red to tell Elaine and Jamie what was going on. The ceremony, he explained, was to make sure the spirits were aware what they were going to try and do and to ask for their guidance – these things, he said, had to be done like they'd always been done, that was the way.

And now especially, because they were going to attempt to step across Time itself, they had to be done properly.

'Simeon calls it a door,' said Red. 'Makes it sound like turning a handle and walking from one room to another, but you saw yesterday how badly it can go wrong.'

'We could turn to *dust*?' Jamie almost whispered the words.

'Dust to dust, just like the old book says.'

Jamie turned and saw Simeon walk back into the room. He was stripped to the waist, with feathers hanging either side of his headband, and was wearing loose buckskin trousers and beaded moccasins. His face and body had been painted with swirling dull red patterns and he was carrying with him a number of unidentifiable things – maybe rattles – and what could have been a tomahawk.

'But it won't happen 'cos you'll all know what you're doing,' said Simeon. 'Now you two can wait outside, this is something just for me 'n Red.'

Outside it was still hot, but at least there was a breeze. Jamie could hear the strange nasal chanting and rhythmic stamping of Simeon and Red doing their ceremony in the candle-lit front room. He found it hard to believe it could have any effect on what they were about to do, but, hey, if he told anyone what they were about to do, they'd think he was crazy as well.

In the calmness of the late afternoon, the sky wide and blue above them and the ground solid beneath their feet, the possibility that someone from another time was doing things that could end up splitting the earth apart seemed completely outrageous. But so was the idea that people from the past could break into the present day. And he'd seen that with his very own eyes.

'Penny for them,' said Elaine.

'What?'

'You day-dreaming, or worried sick? You don't *have* to come, you know.'

'No, I'm not worried.' Jamie stood up and walked down the porch steps. 'Just thinking about stuff, like I'd better make a few calls, straighten this out with my parents.'

Elaine flicked a bug out of her face. 'Sure'.

'I was going to call a friend first,' said Jamie. 'Set something up . . .'

Grabbing the phone he dialled Teejay's private number, which was picked up after two rings. He had a favour to ask, he said, to do with the spur; he knew this would get Teejay interested and it did.

What he wanted to do, he told him, was to tell his parents he was staying over for a couple of days, and to give them his number. All Teej had to do was cover for him if they phoned – could he do that? Sucked into the mystery of the whole thing, Teejay was only too glad to help.

'On one condition,' he said.

'What?' asked Jamie.

'You bring me back some kinda souvenir.'

'You have *no* idea how difficult that could be,' he said. 'But I'll try.'

Jamie had just finished calling home – his mum was out, of course – and leaving a message when Simeon came out of the house. He was covered in sweat and still dressed in his ceremonial costume.

'Right,' he said, 'are you two ready to go?'

'How're we going to get there?' asked Jamie.

'The Chevy.' Red appeared from the house with his backpack.

'What should I do with the Honda?' said Elaine.

'Take it round the back, out of sight.' Simeon nodded at the rear of the house. 'I'll show you where to put it.'

'And where is it we're going, exactly?' asked Elaine.

'The Klamath mountains,' said Simeon. 'Some two hundred miles north of San Francisco.'

'That's two day's away!'

'Now there's two drivers it won't be,' Simeon grinned. 'You'll only have to stop for gas!'

'Great!' said Elaine.

'Your idea to go, not mine.'

'No backing out now.' Elaine went to the Honda and

got in.

While Elaine moved her car, Jamie and Red put all the packs in the back of the truck and then Red reversed it out on to the road. Its engine rumbled like a giant's empty stomach, sounding powerful and not quite tame.

'Will we still be in California?' Jamie asked Red.

'Only just,' he replied. 'We'll be right on the Oregon border, six, seven thousand feet up.'

From the back of the house Simeon and Elaine came into view and walked towards them. Jamie thought Elaine, with her hair pulled back and dressed in Simeon's faded check shirt and patched jeans, looked like a cowgirl or ranch hand – nothing like the sophisticated journalist who had driven up from LA that morning. Checking in the truck's wing mirror he saw himself reflected as a bit of a cowpoke as well.

'OK, time to go,' said Simeon, 'but before you do, there's something I have to give Red.'

Disappearing into the house he came back out a minute or so later holding something in his hand. He reached out to give it to his nephew.

'Take this, and keep it safe,' he said, handing over a small pouch made out of some kind of animal skin, roughly stitched with leather and tied with a thong. 'If you meet him it might make a difference.'

'Thanks.' Red took the pouch and put it in his shirt pocket, buttoning it up.

Before Jamie had a chance to ask what it was – and exactly who they might be meeting – Red was in the truck's cab and revving the engine. Following Elaine round to the passenger door, Jamie got in first and slid across the seat to the middle. Moving the column shift into first gear, Red waved at his uncle and let the clutch out.

The last thing Jamie heard was Simeon calling out 'Good luck!', and the truck was bouncing down the track, a cloud of dust billowing out behind it. They were on the road to yesterday.

By now it was stifling in the warehouse's small office. It had never been intended for anyone to *work* there; it was simply supposed to be used as a safe base and for storage. Charles Dobson had nearly called an office supplies company to get them to deliver a portable air-conditioner, but in the end had decided it wasn't worth the hassle. He and Parnell would just have to sweat it out for as long as it took to set things up.

Using the slush-fund Whelan had provided for buying things there shouldn't be a record of, Dobson ordered everything he thought he might need to get himself back out on the road again. He felt good, his juices were flowing; this was going to be just like the old days and his tracker skills, learned all those years ago in Vietnam, were still as sharp as they'd ever been.

Parnell was on another phone alerting a state-wide string of contacts that he was on the look-out for a certain Honda and its driver – information that he would pay well for. As he was faxing a picture of Elaine McFarlane, scanned from the one used to head her column in the paper, Dobson came off the phone.

'Any news from Tirrel on where her car is?' he asked.

'Let me check.' Parnell dialled a number. 'Tirrel?' he said. 'Well, get him to call me as soon as he comes back . . . thanks.'

'Soon as he gets me the co-ordinates, I'm outta here.'

'Don't hold your breath,' said Parnell, 'she may be out of range, electronics could malfunction – you never know with this stuff.'

'Never had you pegged as a pessimist,' said Dobson, wiping the grease off the unlicensed automatic pistol he'd collected from a safety deposit box he kept for just such items.

'I'm not a pessimist, boss, I'm a *real*ist,' said Parnell, feeding the picture back into the fax machine and dialling a new number. 'Murphy's Law states that "If it can go wrong . . ." '

' " . . . it will go wrong," ' Dobson finished the sentence for him. 'You're right, better to expect nothing and then you won't be disappointed if it doesn't happen, I suppose.'

The phone rang and both men looked at each other, Dobson signalling for his second-in-command to take the call. Parnell grabbed the phone and listened. Then, covering the mouthpiece, he said, 'The tag's working, get a pencil and paper and I'll read you the co-ordinates . . .'

As soon as the call had finished, Parnell opened out a large-scale map of southern California and plotted where

Elaine's car was. 'Way off the beaten track,' he said. 'I wonder what she's doing there?'

'It's not so far from where we saw her yesterday,' said Dobson. 'Maybe that guy she picked up lives there – she might have gone back to see him again.'

'Very possible.' Parnell scratched his head and then checked his watch. 'Tirrel said the car's been there some time, apparently . . . arrived early afternoon and hasn't moved.'

'I'm gone,' said Dobson. He was now dressed in jeans, trainers and a denim shirt; putting the gun in a small shoulder holster he picked up a nylon carry-all and a black leather jacket. 'Keep in touch with Tirrel and let me know if anything happens.'

'OK,' he said, watching Dobson go, 'and enjoy yourself out there.'

'Believe me,' grinned Dobson, 'I will.'

Chapter Fifteen

Timeline: Friday, 5.15pm

Red, it turned out, liked country music. He had a large collection of tapes and a radio that seemed capable of only picking up AM country stations, so there was absolutely nothing else to listen to. After a few hours of heartbreaking stories about sick children, lost love and faithful old dogs that had died tragically, Jamie was of the opinion that, under certain circumstances, going deaf wouldn't be such a bad thing after all. To his utter amazement, Elaine was singing along.

Once they were on the freeway, Red had put his foot down and kept the needle at a steady seventy-five – well over the speed limit. Jamie had pointed this out, but Red assured him everything would be fine as he had radar equipment and a keen eye for speed cops who, he said, if it came to it, he could out-run anyway.

'How fast can this go?' asked Jamie, patting the dashboard.

'I've taken her up to a hundred and twenty,' said Red, 'and I've never had to find out how much more there was left.'

'Well let's keep it a secret, shall we?' said Elaine. 'The whole point is to get there and back alive.'

'What I want to know,' said Jamie, 'is how Simeon knows where this door is, and how he knows where it's going to go – I mean, it all sounds so, I don't know, *random*.'

'The stuff that's going on now *is* random.' Red glanced at him. 'But there are places, sacred places, where the spirits hold a door open. Simeon's been doing a lot of thinking these past few weeks and he's sure he knows who's doing this . . . the only person with the power.'

'So how does he know where it is?'

'He asked the spirits, and they told him.'

Jamie frowned. 'But why do they keep it open?'

'The way Simeon explained it, sometimes things happen – he told me it was almost always real bad things – and the dead can't forget, it's like a trauma.' Red had slowed right down as he spoke. 'The memory of the event is like a scar and it never fades.'

'What happened where we're going?' asked Elaine.

'A massacre, women and children,' he said, 'wiped out by soldiers for no reason.'

Neither of them said anything, they both knew who he meant by 'soldiers' and they both felt more than a little guilty.

The signposts sped by, listing towns and cities Jamie hadn't ever heard of: Delano, Tulare, Chowchilla, Merced, each one full of people who had no idea this beat-up old truck, hurtling northwards, was on a mission that could save their homes, and possibly their lives, from a literally earth-shattering disaster.

Turlock . . . Modesto . . . Manteca . . . the place-names carried on zipping past, but Jamie fell asleep somewhere outside Atwater, just before Red had pulled into a gas station to fill up and let Elaine take over driving. Taking the Yuba City off-ramp, around three in the morning, Elaine stopped and woke Red; he was pleasantly surprised at how far she'd driven and suggested they should park up until dawn and all get some shut-eye.

In a quiet side road, behind a stand of trees, Elaine switched the engine off and they laid Jamie out on the front bench seat. Leaving a window slightly open and locking the doors, she and Red climbed in the back, wrapped themselves in their blankets and fell asleep under the stars.

It wasn't even an hour after the Chevy had disappeared down the track that Simeon saw the dust cloud of a vehicle coming back up. He'd had a feeling he might be having visitors; an ache in his old bones told him trouble was brewing, that and the fact he was sure there'd been another tremor – small, but enough to rattle the crockery in his kitchen, not to mention his nerves.

He was sitting on the porch, Fleet snoozing next to him, whittling a stick with his razor-sharp skinning knife when the car pulled up. It was one of those four-wheel drive cruisers – all wide tyres and bull bars, like a jeep gussied up in a tuxedo. It was Japanese – not that Simeon had anything against the Japanese; it was just that he was of the opinion they couldn't build big old dirt-busters like they could in Detroit, was all.

The car rocked to a halt and Simeon watched the man inside get out. He was in his late forties, well-built, muscular and quite fit looking; he was wearing jeans and a short-waisted leather jacket and he walked like a boxer – light on his feet for a man of his size and age. But there was something about him that made Simeon think he should've been wearing a suit and tie. His haircut, maybe.

The man walked towards him, hands in his jeans pockets, eyes scanning where the Chevy had been parked. He stopped at the foot of the stairs leading up to the porch.

'Lost your way?' enquired Simeon.

'Not as far as I know,' replied Dobson. 'I'm looking for a Ms Elaine McFarlane . . . I'm told she might be here.'

'And who might have told you that?'

'A friend of mine.'

'Your friend say why he thought that?' Simeon looked straight at Dobson, but carried on whittling.

'Her car, a Honda, was seen coming up this way,' said Dobson, 'and no-one's seen it leave.'

'Your friend's eyesight needs checking, she left some time ago.' This information didn't seem to come as a surprise to Simeon's visitor and his eyes wandered over the house for a moment before he spoke again.

'Could you tell me where she went?' he said finally.

'No idea.'

'Mind if I look around?'

'To tell you the honest truth, I wouldn't mind if you moved in, mister, but Fleet here,' Simeon indicated the big black dog now sitting up next to him, 'he just *hates* strangers.'

Fleet remained stock still, staring right at Dobson, a slight quiver in his soft muzzle the only sign of movement. Dobson ignored the dog, his right hand reaching into his jacket.

'If I were you,' said Simeon, a low, evil growl rolling up out of Fleet's throat, 'I wouldn't do that, mister.'

'I simply wanted to give you my card,' explained Dobson, slowly dropping his hand. If the old man wanted to play it tough, that was fine by him. His fighting days had started back in '70, behind the lines in Cambodia during 'Nam; he might look like a friendly middle-aged guy, but he'd been taught more ways to kill than there were to cook eggs. 'You can give it to her when she comes back – I need to talk to her.'

'What makes you think she'll be back?'

'To get her car.'

Simeon's eyes momentarily flicked over his shoulder, and Dobson caught the look.

'You have *no* idea who you're dealing with,' he said.

'Mister,' said Simeon, standing up, the dog's growl changing up a gear as he did so, 'whatever game it is you're playing, it's a side-show to what's waiting in the wings . . . believe me.'

Dobson grinned. 'I don't have time to play,' he said,

turning to walk back to the car. 'And rest assured, wherever she's gone, I'll find her.'

'Don't bet on it.'

Dobson heard the dog's claws on the porch steps. 'He comes near me, he's dead meat,' he said without looking back, his voice suddenly very steely. There was the sound of fingers clicking and the dog stopped.

Getting into the Toyota Landcruiser Dobson did a three-point turn and floored the accelerator, sending a hail of small stones out behind him. Standing on the porch Simeon saw that the Toyota had a serious-looking trail bike racked on the back of it. This guy, he thought, is covering *all* his bases.

The Landcruiser pitched and yawed down the track, and it wasn't until he'd had made it to the road that Dobson was able to use the car phone to get in touch with Parnell.

He picked up immediately. 'Everything OK, boss?' he asked.

'Sure.'

'What happened?'

'She's not at the house,' said Dobson. 'I saw some tracks, a big four-wheel drive, she must've gone with the other guy you saw.'

'I was talking to a cop I know, works up there where you are. He gave me a name – Red Stonegarden – and the licence plate of the Chevy truck he drives.' Parnell waited for Dobson to say something, but he didn't. 'I put them out on the wire and they've been spotted going north on the freeway.'

'Fine,' said Dobson, curtly. 'Let me know when you hear anything else – I'm on my way.' Cutting the phone he smiled. Things were working out just fine.

Chapter Sixteen

Timeline: Saturday, 9.25am

The road had all but run out. They were now so high up that birds, looking a lot like eagles, were flying level with them far out in the valley. They'd woken at sun-up – without a watch Jamie had no idea exactly what the time was – and gone to a twenty-four-hour truck stop for breakfast and then set off. Now the driving was over, and the rest of the way they'd have to do by foot.

Red parked the truck behind some bushes and locked it. After he and Jamie had done their best to hide it with some cut branches, they picked up their blanket rolls and began to walk. The Klamath mountain range was beautiful in the early morning, and for the first hour Jamie enjoyed tramping behind Elaine as Red took the lead. He didn't seem to have a map and appeared to be following his nose, but then, thought Jamie, he was a Nez Percés and maybe that's how they did things.

As the sun crawled up the sky, burning off what clouds there were, Jamie broke out his water bottle, only to be told he should be careful – what they were carrying, said Red, was all they had until they came across a stream.

'How much further is it?' asked Jamie who, being a true

LA kid, wasn't used to walking even down the end of the road, let alone half way over a mountain.

'Another hour, maybe an hour and a half,' came the reply.

And on they went.

From going uphill, the path they were on, if you could call it that, began to take a downward turn, snaking into a small shadow-laden, mist-filled valley that you had to know was there to find. The air cooled considerably as they went down amongst the overhangs, and then Red suddenly stopped.

'Look,' he said, pointing into the valley. 'There it is.'

'I can't see anything,' said Elaine, taking her sunglasses off. 'And anyway, what am I supposed to be looking *for*?'

Red sketched a kind of arch in front of him with his index finger. 'The door,' he said. 'See the shimmering, like there was a fire down there?'

Jamie shaded his eyes, wishing he'd got his binoculars with him, and then he saw it – a place where the air seemed like the glass in a bathroom window. 'Got it!'

'Well I *still* can't see it.' Elaine put her sunglasses back on again. 'Let's get down there and have a proper look, shall we?'

The three of them made their way down the final hundred metres or so to the valley floor and picked their way over the boulders and rocks that lay on it, as if carelessly tossed. Red stopped some five metres from the rippling space and, fascinated, Jamie walked past him to have a closer look.

'Careful!'

Jamie stopped and stared. In front of him was the door, the time gate; he hadn't known what to expect – in all the excitement hadn't really given it that much thought – but standing there, faced with it, all he could think to say was 'Awesome . . .', which hardly began to describe its fragile beauty.

It was a lazy shape, not solid, not actually liquid either, and it kind of *billowed* like a sail, the glassy air seeming almost alive. It was about two metres in height and some metre and a half wide and Jamie realized that he now had a high-pitched buzzing in his ears, the sort you got after listening to very loud music for too long. And there was a smell, an electric freshness that pricked his nose.

'And Simeon's taught you how to do this properly?' Jamie heard Elaine ask.

'Sure hope so.'

'Glad you're so sure, Red . . . it makes me feel a whole lot better.'

Elaine's sarcasm was lost on Red, who was also staring at the door. Jamie went back over to where Elaine was standing and they both watched him. In the silence it felt like he was standing in the ruins of some gigantic church, and he felt intimidated and impressed at the same time, nervous with the anticipation of what they were going to do.

Red turned to face them. 'Now's the time to figure if you *really* want to go on,' he said quietly. 'You don't have to come. I'll give you the keys and you can drive back to Simeon's if you want.'

'You think I'm scared, or something?' said Elaine.

'You should be, cos I am.'

'OK, I admit it, so am I, but that's never prevented me from doing anything before,' Elaine put a hand on Jamie's shoulder. 'And anyway, I don't think we really have a choice – staying here isn't an option, too dangerous by half, and you heard the news report about the tremor yesterday . . . it's going to happen if we don't stop it, Red.'

'How about you?' Red asked Jamie.

'I'm, you know, *fine*,' he said, although scared wasn't really the word he'd have used to explain how he felt. It was more along the lines of petrified. But having come this far, walked all that way, there was *no* way he wasn't going through with the whole thing. 'Don't worry about me.'

'Good, because you're going first.' Red beckoned him over. 'Walk steady, and whatever you do, don't stop – Elaine'll be right behind you, and wher*ever* you come out, just hit the dirt and stay there until I join you – got that?'

'Don't stop . . . hit the dirt . . .'

'Straight down.'

Jamie took a deep breath. 'What do I do now?'

'Stand in front of the door, hold your pack in front of you, keep your shoulders in tight and walk right through the middle.' Red carefully lined him up, and Elaine noticed him mutter something under his breath.

'Shall I go?' asked Jamie.

'If it feels good, do it.'

Jamie picked up his blanket roll and hugged it like it was his mother, curving his shoulders round till his muscles ached. 'Right,' he said. 'I'm off!'

Not daring to blink, he walked forward. As he got closer to the door, the buzzing in his ears got louder and the air in front of him seemed to boil, without being hot. On he went, the buzzing sounding like his dad's electric razor, the weird frosted glass effect getting stronger until it was all he could see. And then he was in it. *In* the doorway.

His feet still felt like they were on the ground, but for all he knew he could be floating. His spine tingled as he felt a coldness run down it, and his hair stood up. The smell was now very strong, and when he looked down he saw his left foot go forward and disappear out of the wavering mist and he nearly stopped walking. Then he remembered what Red had told him and forced himself on.

And, quite suddenly, he was out in the bright sunshine, standing on a dusty, scrub-covered hillside somewhere completely else. He was so surprised that, even if Red hadn't told him to do it, he felt like he would have fallen over anyway.

Parnell's call had woken Dobson at about half past six. For a moment he hadn't known where he was, and the motel room, in a place some way north of Sacramento, had given him no clues at all. Shaking the sleep from his head he picked up the warbling mobile on the bedside table and answered it.

'Yup . . .'

'Rise and shine, boss – I've got another fix on them.' Parnell sounded like he'd been up for hours. 'They've got the kid with them as well.'

Dobson walked into the bathroom and turned on the shower. 'A happy little band,' he said. 'Where are they?'

'They had breakfast at a truck stop near Yuba City, then got back on the freeway and headed north . . . about an hour and fifteen minutes ago.'

'Any idea of their destination?'

'My contact said the kid was heard asking how far the Klamath mountains were,' said Parnell. 'Best I can do.'

'Give me a complete description of the truck,' said Dobson, running a hand through his tousled hair. 'I'll find 'em . . . and, Parnell?'

'Yeah boss?'

'How far ahead are they?'

'An hour, maybe less – if you're lucky.'

'I intend to be,' said Dobson. 'Talk to you later.'

CHAPTER SEVENTEEN

Timeline: Saturday afternoon, exact time unknown

The sun shone, so bright and hard it was almost physical. Lying on the parched ground, with Elaine and Red on either side of him, Jamie peered through the low branches of the dry, thorny bush they were hiding behind. No-one had said a word since they'd all arrived and moved some way from the door.

Below them came the sound of voices – shouting, cajoling, yelling back and forth – and under that the low rumble of iron-bound wheels being pulled slowly over uneven rocks. The men Jamie could see were dressed in dark blue uniforms and wore wide-brimmed hats, high leather boots and most were carrying rifles; a number rode on horseback, the rest walked in a straggly column in front of lurching, rolling canvas-topped wagons and a line of wheeled cannon.

'The *army?*' whispered Jamie, eyes wide open, mouth agape.

Red glanced his way. 'Down there, somewhere near the front, should be Colonel Jefferson Davis,' he said, 'commander-in-chief and all-round hard man.'

'How d'you know that?' Jamie asked.

'Simeon made me read up on where I'd be going.'

'Where are we?' said Jamie, still whispering even though there was no way the soldiers far below could have heard him.

'North of where we were, in the Cascades,' replied Red.

'I think Jamie meant where in *time*,' said Elaine.

'Late May, 1873.'

'Wow!' exclaimed Jamie. *'Really?'*

Elaine shifted forward to get a better view. 'And what is Colonel Jefferson Davis up to? Where's he taking these guys – out on exercise?'

Red shook his head. 'Nope, he's going into battle . . . we're right in the middle of the Modoc War.'

'What is that when it's at home?' Jamie shuffled about to make himself more comfortable on the hard ground. 'Something like Vietnam?'

'A lot shorter,' Red rolled sideways and propped himself up on one arm. 'According to Simeon, it lasted, ooh, some seven, eight months only – but it was big news all the same.'

'Why?' asked Jamie.

'Hardly more than fifty men held off a US Army force of maybe a thousand troops, up near Lake Tule . . . somewhere called Land of the Burnt-Out Fires. Sent them running for their sorry lives,' Red shook his head. 'Then, when he was *supposed* to be talking peace, their leader, Kintpuash – or Captain Jack, as the whites called him – killed General Canby. Shot him right in the face, the only man of his rank ever to be killed in the whole of the Indian Wars. That's why they sent Davis after him; the government wasn't about to be shown up by a bunch of no-account hunters.'

Elaine asked, 'Why did Simeon want you to come back here, to this time, Red?'

'He says this is where the powerful medicine man is, the one who's trying another method of getting back at the white man and his bad ways . . . you know, rather than fighting.' Red shrugged. 'Sounds reasonable to me. Fighting never got us anywhere but on a reservation.'

Jamie had done some work at school on the Indian Wars, and knew how terribly the tribes had been treated – and cheated. In class he'd thought it very unfair, but now, out here and with Red, he felt ashamed of his heritage.

'You two should stay put, out of sight.' Red looked down at the seemingly endless stream of men and guns, and then up the hill behind him. 'I have to go for a while.'

'Can we move into the shade?' Elaine pointed at an overhang, back to the left. 'We'll still be hidden.'

'That's fine.' Red opened up his blanket roll and Jamie saw it contained a couple of things he hadn't seen before – an old Colt .45 and a leather belt and holster. He watched Red check the pistol, slide it into the holster and strap the belt, heavy with extra bullets, round his waist.

'Is that Simeon's?'

'My granddaddy's.'

'It work?' asked Elaine.

'Last time I fired it.' Red got up into a crouch, grinned, waved and moved off without another word.

Jamie watched him dodge from bush to bush, and then he was gone. 'Can you believe we're here?' he said.

'Hardly,' said Elaine. 'Except I'm hot, dusty and wildly uncomfortable . . . and somehow I'm positive there isn't a cold bottle of imported beer within a hundred and fifty years of this place.'

Without a watch neither of them had any real idea how long Red was gone. The sun moved some way across the sky and, when the last of Colonel Davis's troops disappeared round the bend in the trail that took it out of the valley, a heavy silence fell. The heat made it difficult to talk, or even think, and the two of them lay down and spent their time resting; Elaine had actually dozed off at one point, waking with a start when Jamie sneezed.

'Sorry, dust up my nose,' he said.

'Any sign of Red?'

'No . . . no sign of anyone or anything, now the soldiers are gone.'

'I hope nothing's happened to him,' sighed Elaine. 'If we have to go back through that door on our own there's no telling *where* we'd end up – in the middle of some primeval soup, knowing my luck and sense of direction.'

'If I had a choice, it'd be Hollywood in the Forties,' grinned Jamie. 'I love all those old black and white gangster movies!'

'Nah!' said Elaine, joining in the game, 'I'd go back to

the Fifties, find Elvis and tell him to take better care of himself, otherwise he'll die fat and too young!'

They both started giggling hysterically, the tension that had held them firmly in its grip for the last twenty-four hours finally breaking. It felt good to laugh; it allowed them to forget where they were for a moment and relax.

A loud crunching sound, that of leather hitting stony ground, preceded a tall shadow falling in front of them. 'Quiet, guys . . . you never know who's listening out here,' said a voice, and then Red was standing in front of them. 'Time to go,' he beckoned them up.

'Where?' Jamie scrambled to his feet, slightly embarrassed at being caught fooling around.

'I got some horses over the rise . . . and some help.'

'Help?' queried Elaine. 'You have *friends* around here?'

'I do now.'

'How come?' Elaine picked up her roll and looked round the overhang to see if there was anyone there.

'I made contact with some of my own tribe, four of them.' Red took the roll Jamie handed him. 'They think I've got the spirit in me, and I told them we needed help.'

'You can talk to them?' asked Elaine, following after Red as he began to walk up the hill.

'Simeon taught me . . . we get by.'

'And just who do they think *we* are?'

'Good guys.'

CHAPTER EIGHTEEN

Timeline: Saturday, later

Jamie felt his heart pounding, not from the exertion of clambering up the hill with his backpack, but at the thought of what was waiting over the rise – four Nez Percés tribesmen with, Red had told them, three extra horses. He was a fairly accomplished rider, on a well-trained horse with a saddle, but here he'd likely have to ride bareback. And not fall off.

They topped the hill and some way down, waiting in under a tree, he saw them squatting in the shade. Four men, quite small, dressed in loose shirts and what looked like baggy cotton trousers, their long black hair hanging over their shoulders in braids. No magnificent feathered head-dresses, no wampum beads and not a tomahawk in sight. A part of him was disappointed.

As they made their way down, Jamie saw a number of horses tethered to a nearby tree. They weren't like the sleek, well-groomed mounts he'd ridden at the stables. These creatures were not so big and were, if he remembered correctly, probably mustangs. None of them had saddles, just patterned blankets on their backs, and, he thought, if he ached a little now from all the walking, he was going to ache a whole lot more once they set off on their journey.

Red loped towards the men, leaving Elaine and Jamie to walk slowly behind him, and they watched as the Nez Percés got up as he approached. There was no hand-shaking as they met, just a slight nod of their heads – they seemed courteous, almost respectful, and Jamie wondered what Red had told them to make them act that way. He and Elaine stopped a few metres from the group and waited to be introduced.

Whatever they were talking about, the conversation went on for ages, one or other of the men occasionally glancing their way.

'D'you think this is all about us?' Jamie muttered under his breath, looking at Elaine.

'I don't think so,' she said. 'Look . . .'

Jamie turned and saw one of the men was now kneeling on the ground, using a stick to draw something in the dust. 'A map?' he said.

'Most likely,' Elaine nodded, watching him scratch what had to be mountains and then a squiggly line – meant, she supposed, to be a river.

'I'm gonna sit down,' said Jamie, dropping his backpack and plonking himself down on it with a sigh. One of the Nez Percés looked over at him and smiled, his teeth brown and snaggled, his skin a deeply burnished brown. Not red at all, thought Jamie, shyly smiling back.

Elaine joined him, electing to sit cross-legged, leaning forward on the rolled blanket on her lap. 'This is just like when I was a kid,' she said. 'Every year we'd all pile into my dad's Dodge station wagon and set off for some damn place or other he'd heard about from a friend . . . and he'd always have to stop and spend hours yelling at a deaf gas station owner trying to figure out where he'd taken a wrong turning. If he wasn't deaf he'd be half-blind . . . always something.'

'My dad plans a holiday like a military invasion,' said Jamie. '08.00 hours, leave house . . . 08.35, turn left on to Ventura . . .'

'We never had a plan, just a general direction and a big cool-box full of snacks.' Elaine shook her head at the memory. 'A chaotic way to travel, but it had the advantage of never being boring . . . hey, looks like we're about to move, Jamie boy.'

Red stood up and stretched, the four Nez Percés standing as well, the one with the stick using his foot to rub out the map. Red said something to his new friends, something that sounded like it had the words 'Elaine' and 'Jamie' in it, and the men looked over at them. 'Time for introductions,' he said as they both got up. 'They speak a very little English, but they've got trading post names, which'll be easier for everyone.'

Going from left to right he pointed to Tin-can Charley, Cold Abe, Hookey Joe and finally Boots Franklin, the map drawer, each nodding as he said their name. And that was it. Boots, who seemed to act as kind of leader, took the others off to get the horses.

'How'd they get such odd names?' asked Jamie.

'Good old boys who run the trading posts can mostly never be bothered to learn their real ones,' explained Red.

'They just give them whatever comes to mind instead. Sometimes it's like a nickname description, sometimes not . . . I didn't ask these guys which it was with them.'

'Well I'm sure, after seeing *me* ride, they'll not be lost for a nickname or two,' grinned Elaine. 'Last time I was on a horse it had a pole sticking right through it and only went round in circles to calliope music.'

'Don't worry, we'll be taking it fairly easy,' said Red. 'And these horses, they've almost got automatic transmission.'

'I'll be clutching, nonetheless.'

They rode until the sun went down, a dull red ball that sank, almost groaning, into an intense pink, then glorious purple bed of the horizon. It was a truly amazing sight, out there in the wilds of Oregon, miles from anywhere, a timeless flight from home – a sight Jamie knew he'd never forget, no matter how long he lived.

Riding the small rugged horses had been a lot easier than he'd thought it would be; you had to sit further forward than you would if there'd been a saddle, gripping round the curve of the horse's belly, and doing little else than keeping a loose hold of the simple reins.

Before darkness fell completely Boots stopped the party close to a river. The four Nez Percés tethered their horses and melted away into the trees that sheltered them.

'Where're they going?' asked Jamie.

'Get some supper.'

'Anything we can do?' said Elaine, massaging her gently aching back.

'Get some wood so's we can cook whatever they catch?' suggested Red. 'We're going to stay here the night, leave Silver Heart till tomorrow.'

'Silver Heart – is that the place we're going?' asked Jamie. Red shuddered, and Jamie thought that if his mother had been there she would have commented that an angel must have walked on his grave; he'd always found it a really weird thing for her to say, but now he could see what she meant.

'Silver Heart's a person, Jamie,' he said at last. 'He's a shaman, a medicine man – Simeon says the most powerful there ever was.'

'If he's responsible for what's been going on,' said Elaine, 'then I'd say Simeon was about right. How near are we?'

'We're there,' said Red. 'It's just over the rise.'

'Why're we waiting then?'

'This is something I want to do by daylight, Elaine . . .'

Chapter Nineteen

Timeline: Saturday night

By the time they had a fire going it was pitch dark and the night sky was littered with so many stars it looked like someone had spilt flour on a massive piece of black velvet. Nights in LA were nothing like this, the city glow masking out so much of what was up there. Jamie had watched, spellbound, as Red had used the contents of his tinderbox to light the fire, first shredding the softest, driest wood he could find, then striking the flint until he had the first feeble glimmerings. Within minutes flames licked the air, and not long afterwards he'd banked up a serious fire, its smoke rising as a column in the cool stillness.

They'd not had to wait long before Boots and the others were back, Hookey with a small deer slung over his shoulder. By the light of the fire he soon had the animal skinned, gutted and on a spit, resting on two forked sticks above the flames. Elaine hadn't been able to watch, muttering something about it being enough to turn you vegetarian and going off to look at the river. The aroma of cooked deer dragged her back to the fireside, and she didn't turn down the hunk of meat Cold Abe offered her on a 'plate' made out of a large leaf. Whether it was simply hunger, or a combination of exercise, fresh air and sheer elation at being where they were, both Elaine and Jamie agreed they'd never eaten food that tasted so good.

They'd bedded down in a tight circle round the fire, the horses tethered close to them, and Jamie was out like a light. He woke, while it was still dark, to find everyone else was up, Boots and the others standing in a group while Elaine crouched over Red.

'What is it, Red?' he heard Elaine say. 'Are you all right?'

Jamie stood up. 'What's happening?' he asked drowsily, a little unsteady on his feet.

'He's having some kind of nightmare – his eyes are open, but I can't seem to wake him.'

'What's he saying?'

'Can't quite make it out . . . something about forces . . . forces being pushed . . .'

Boots Franklin detached himself from the others and step by step came over next to Jamie. 'Sick,' he said, pointing at Red.

'No,' said Jamie, 'no, he's not sick . . . it's, you know, like a dream – bad dream?'

Boots frowned, shaking his head as he said something to the others, and Jamie suddenly remembered where he was, who he was talking to. These people didn't think the way he did; they believed different things in a completely different way.

'It's OK,' he said, as calmly as he could. 'He's fine,

just tired, very tired.' He did a pantomime of ragged exhaustion and pointed to Red.

'I think he's waking,' said Elaine over her shoulder.

Jamie moved over to her side and saw that Red was sitting up, his face a deathly pale in the silver moonlight. 'He looks awful,' he whispered.

'He's hot, almost a fever,' said Elaine, leaning forward and patting his cheek. And then Red blinked and he stared up at Elaine as if he'd never seen her before in his life. 'He's back,' she said.

Red rubbed his face with both hands, as if trying to wipe away the memory of what he'd just been through. He sat for a long time, silent, rocking slightly to and fro, his hands still massaging his temples. 'Bad one,' he finally said. 'Real bad.'

'What happened?' asked Elaine, helping him up and nodding at Jamie to get her a water flask.

'The closer we get, the stronger I feel it.'

'Feel what?'

'I suppose you could call it the magic.'

From somewhere in the dark someone, Jamie thought it was Tin-can, said something and Red, taking the flask, spoke back, his voice low. He talked for some time, his free hand acting like an extra mouth, presumably explaining to the tribesmen what had happened. And then, taking a long drink, he shivered and got up. 'They're worried,' he said to Elaine. 'They think I'm possessed by an evil spirit.'

'What did you tell them? she asked.

'I told them it wasn't an *evil* spirit, just a troubled one that needed to talk.'

Jamie noticed a faint pinkness to the eastern horizon, and the growing light of the approaching dawn gave some much-needed colour to Red's cheeks. 'Do they believe you?' he said.

'These guys don't know *what* to believe,' said Red. 'They know all about Silver Heart and are probably more scared of him than me right now.'

'Want to rest some more?' said Elaine.

'We better get going.' Red stamped his feet to get warmer. 'Have some food and move out . . . they think it's, like, haunted round here.'

Elaine looked at him. 'Yeah . . .' she said, 'I believe I know what they mean.'

Jamie, who'd been concentrating on what Red had been saying, had forgotten about the others. Then he heard Boots yell something; turning he saw he was up on his horse, wrenching his mount sideways, kicking hard with his heels. The horse knew what to do and curved out into the tall grass and was away at a gallop; Hookey and the rest were scrambling on to their rides and making good their escape.

'Where are they going?' Elaine sounded slightly panicked at the sight of the Nez Percés taking off so suddenly.

'Away from the angry spirits,' muttered Red.

'Angry *spirits*!' yelled Elaine, blowing wisps of hair out of her face as she bent forward, her face only inches from

Red's. 'What is going *on*, Red? Why'd they really run away like that?'

Red shook his head, still with that odd smile on his face. 'I meant what I said; we're close to the source of all this . . . close to Silver Heart . . . and they were spooked, big time. Anyway, like I told you, we're here . . . we don't need 'em any more.'

Without their guides for company Jamie felt lonelier than he'd ever felt in his whole life. Lonely and exposed; nowhere to run, nowhere to hide. After the events of the last twenty-four hours, Jamie wondered about whatever could possibly happen next. Would they be in time to stop Silver Heart? Or, when they went back, would LA be a smoking ruin?

As soon as the sun was fully up, Red led them up the lightly wooded slopes of the small valley they'd camped in. He moved with a grace and quietness that Jamie found uncanny; it was like watching an animal – a fox or a big cat – out hunting. By comparison he and Elaine were elephants.

At the valley's edge the ground fell away gently to a wide plain. In the middle of the vast open space, what looked to be a half a mile away from where they lay, they could make out a large encampment, dozens of thin trails of wood smoke rising from the cluster of teepees.

'Mysteriouser and mysteriouser,' said Elaine.

'He's there?' asked Jamie.

'In person.'

'He's sitting in his teepee, in the middle of nowhere in 1873, and lobbing time bombs – if you'll pardon the pun – over a *hundred years* into the future?' said Elaine. 'Did good old Simeon tell you how, by any chance?'

Red slid back down the slope and got up. 'He's made a mistake.'

'No kidding!'

'Don't mock what you don't understand, Elaine.' Red's eyes narrowed and he looked angry. 'Whatever this man is doing, he's doing it to save his people . . . Simeon says it's gone wrong because the earth spirits Silver Heart has called up are far more powerful than even *he* realized.'

'I apologize for being flippant, I guess I'm a little spooked myself,' said Elaine. 'What are you going to do?'

'Try and get him to stop.' Red turned and started walking back towards the camp site.

'Where are you going?' said Jamie.

'I've got to get myself ready to meet him . . . meet Silver Heart – stay here, and keep well down.'

They both did as they were told, and for the next five or so minutes they watched the encampment. When they got bored they went back down to see what Red was up to, but he was nowhere to be seen. His horse had been stripped of its blanket and it was tethered apart from the other two. Jamie was checking the small pile of bed rolls, and had just found Red's shirt, when he saw a figure coming towards him through the trees. For a second he didn't recognize who it was.

'Red?' he called out. 'That you?'

'Uh-huh,' came the reply.

'Where've you been?' asked Elaine.

'Fixing myself up.'

Jamie stared at him in amazement. 'Fixing himself up' meant he'd tied his long hair back and coated it with mud, covering his whole body from the waist up in blue – almost black – patterns. The last time they'd seen him he'd looked like a regular twentieth-century guy; now he was every bit a true Plains warrior.

Chapter Twenty

Timeline: Sunday morning

'Impressive,' said Elaine. 'Why the war paint?'

Red went over to where Jamie was standing holding his shirt. 'It's not war paint,' he said, reaching out and taking it from him. 'These are tribal markings that Silver Heart should recognize – make him realize I'm a friend.'

Opening one of the shirt pockets, Red took out the small pouch Simeon had given him and tucked it into his jeans.

'What *is* that?' asked Jamie.

Red took the reins off his horse. 'Something to convince him, if he doesn't believe me.'

'How're you going to ride, without the reins and blanket?'

'The old way,' replied Red, leading the horse up the hill.

Out on the plains the encampment sat in a shimmer of heat-haze, one or two wisps of smoke rising into the sky from fires. The whole scene looked like a huge painting.

'I suppose we wait here,' said Elaine.

'Best to do that,' agreed Red.

Jamie watched as he lay forward on the horse, sliding

down and clinging to its side like a limpet on a seaside rock. For a moment Jamie couldn't work out what he was doing and then, as Red urged the horse away, becoming a dark shape against grass, he saw exactly why. To the casual observer it looked just like a riderless horse galloping across the plains – and Red would be almost at the camp before a look-out could possibly spot him.

He and Elaine watched him go; they waited until Red's path took him to the outside edge of the teepee circle and then saw him jump to the ground. He was so far away now that it was impossible to make out what kind of reception he got and the two of them went back down to the camp to wait.

Red knew his approach wouldn't have gone unnoticed; a lone horse making its way towards the camp was bound to cause a flurry of excitement. When he coaxed his mount to a halt some twenty metres from the perimeter and slid to the ground he saw half a dozen warriors waiting for him, three of them with bowstrings pulled taut, arrows aimed straight at his chest. Standing stock still he heard the sound of quiet feet whisper through the grass as men took up position behind him.

'I come in peace,' he said. 'I come to speak with Silver Heart.'

'Who talks?' said one of the warriors, moving closer to him.

'Red Stonegarden.'

There was a long pause after Red spoke, and he could

hear muttering. 'This name means nothing to us,' said the same voice.

'Maybe not, but I have a message to pass on.' Red held his arms out, palms to the blue sky. 'I am unarmed, and the spirits walk at my side – Silver Heart *will* want to speak with me.'

There was another muffled conversation, and finally the warrior nearest him motioned him forward and they walked through the outer circle of tents and into the camp itself. Red saw them looking at his tribal markings – the ones Simeon had spent so long teaching him how to put on. Nervously he waited to find out if he'd learnt his lessons well.

After a short discussion Elaine and Jamie had decided it would be best if they didn't light a fire. It might attract attention of the wrong kind. They ate what was left of the deer and some of the dried meat, drank a little water and by the time they'd finished Elaine was yawning.

'I didn't get enough shut-eye last night,' she said, rubbing her eyes.

'I'll keep a watch for a bit,' said Jamie, who still felt quite alert. 'You bed down.'

'Wake me in an hour or so,' she grinned sleepily, unrolling her blanket and pulling it round her.

It seemed to Jamie that, almost before her head had touched the ground, Elaine was out for the count. He sat and watched her face, half in shadow, wondering what good keeping watch would do if he hadn't got anything to protect them with (Protect them from what? said a small voice in his head. Bears? Wolves? Marauding tribesmen?). And then he remembered the pistol.

Red hadn't been wearing his holster when he left, so it must still be in his backpack. He went and got it, undoing the straps and rolling the blanket out. There it was, a dull glint reflecting off the greased silver-grey metal; he picked the holster up, surprised at how heavy it was, and strapped it round his waist.

It felt weird to be wearing a real gun, fully loaded, ready to use. Reared on a diet of old cowboy movies and new cop shows, guns were as much a part of life as cars – at least as toys. But this was the genuine thing, a bona fide firearm that was heavy with mortality.

Strangely enough, sitting alone in the wilderness, he felt much better with the Colt's weight hanging by his side. He didn't take it out – it wasn't something to be played with – but as he sat, his back up against a tree, his right hand was never more than a few inches from its wooden grip. An odd kind of comfort.

Whatever the warriors surrounding Red saw, it obviously satisfied them that he wasn't a threat. He'd waited, silent and ram-rod straight, as they'd looked him over for some time and then the only one who'd spoken to him directly so far had told him to follow, turning and walking into the hub of the encampment.

Red tried to keep as calm as possible as he walked, but it was hard; here he was among his ancestors, in a world he knew so well from his uncle's stories. His family had always accused Simeon of having one foot in the past, and here *he* was, actually there. He saw his progress was being watched by a growing crowd of silent people; word of his arrival, a painted stranger from out of the grasslands, must have spread like wildfire through the camp. By the time he reached a large teepee at the centre of the circle, he knew every soul in the place, man, woman and child, would be there too.

For all the tension he felt, his muscles bunched, taut, as if ready to run – though he knew there was nowhere he could go – there was a certain calmness in the air. It hung, like the mist and seemed to be damping down the unease, even hostility, these people must be feeling. A rustle of whispers ran, like autumn leaves in the breeze, through the watching crowd as the doorway to the big teepee opened and an old man, white hair in two long braids hanging over his shoulders, stooped through the gap and came out.

Silver Heart, thought Red; it had to be.

He stood, feet slightly apart, hands clasped in front of him, with his head bowed and waited for the old man to speak. It was the way. It showed respect.

A surprisingly strong voice asked: 'Who do we welcome to our fire?'

'I am named after Red Echo, greatest of the Nez Percés chiefs . . . I am called Red Stonegarden.'

Silver Heart stared at Red through half-shut, slitted eyes and he felt as if the old man was actually trying to look inside him for the truth – or otherwise – of his words. It was unnerving, like watching a doctor peer at your X-rays, searching for something wrong. Finally he spoke. 'You speak the right words,' he said, 'but you don't quite say them in the proper way . . . you look like a dream I once had, real, yet not of *this* world.'

'He said the spirits walked at his side,' said the warrior who'd led him in.

'Did he?' said Silver Heart, looking away for a moment. 'Which world are you from, stranger?'

'Tomorrow,' Red replied.

'How can this be?' asked Silver Heart.

Red slowly reached into his jeans pocket and pulled out the leather pouch. He held it by the thong and let in dangle in the air in front of him. 'I bring you back something you haven't yet made,' he said.

Jamie thought he might have fallen asleep himself; he couldn't remember. But his neck ached, probably from having fallen forward, his backside was numb and he desperately needed to take a leak. Getting up he checked on Elaine and found her curled up in a tight ball, dead to the world.

Even though there was no-one else nearer than the encampment, Jamie, through force of habit, made his way through the trees until he was some way from where Elaine slept. Better safe than sorry.

Once he'd finished, and finally managed to get the button-fly closed (no wonder they invented zips, he thought), he started back. He was being quiet, the way you are when you're on edge, even when you don't have to be, when he thought he heard something and jerked his head around. Nothing. And then he saw it – someone creeping through the trees way to his right. He froze and held his breath. The silent shadowy figure carried on moving, following, it looked like, the path they'd come up themselves the day before. Making his way towards Elaine.

Jamie's heart felt like it was about to burst, and he let his breath out in a low hiss. What should he do? Shout out and warn her? That could be a big mistake; what if whoever it was didn't run away and came for him instead? His brain fought to sort out all the possibilities and probabilities, to make some kind of sense of what was happening and what he should do. Somewhere in the back of his mind a little piece of information was yelling out to him: *think of the games you play on the computer!* it said.

Renegade Warrior was his favourite of the moment, and a quiet stealth was needed to get through the levels without being trashed by all the ghouls and demons lying in wait. You often had to creep up on them and surprise them in order to make a kill. Not that he ever wanted to kill anyone, but he did want to surprise the person now only a few metres away from the horses.

It was the horses that allowed Jamie to shadow the figure without being heard; they started snorting and moving nervously as he (it didn't look like a woman . . . didn't, now he came to think of it, look like a Nez Percés or any other kind of tribesman) came near them and then went past. Jamie watched as the man scanned their simple campsite, taking in the two bedrolls, and Elaine's sleeping form.

Nervous as a canary at a cat convention, Jamie stopped; it was no good having a gun if it stayed put in its holster. His hand damp with sweat he gingerly removed it – what was it he'd heard someone say in a film once: never take your gun out unless you intend to use it? The thought almost made him slide it back into its leather home, but he didn't and crept out of the trees and nearer the man.

His arm was shaking slightly as he raised the pistol, and he used his left hand to steady his aim, the barrel pointing right at the middle of the man's broad back. It was then he noticed he was wearing trainers. '*Wha . . . ?*' he spluttered.

The man swung round. It was a graceful move for someone so large, almost like a ballet dancer; the man's leg arced up and round in a vicious kick that sent the Colt flying out of Jamie's hands and flung him sideways. He hit the ground hard.

'OK, kid,' he heard a gruff voice say as he picked himself up, 'get over with your friend.'

'Who are you?' said Elaine, eyes fixed on the man now pointing an automatic at her.

'Kneel on the ground, both of you,' snarled the man, 'hands behind your back.'

Jamie did as he was told; his hand hurt and he felt woozy from the fall. He glanced sideways at Elaine.

'I asked who you were,' she said through gritted teeth.

'Charles Dobson,' the man replied.

Chapter Twenty-One

Timeline: Sunday, late morning

Elaine tried hard not to look surprised, shocked even, at discovering that the man standing over them with a gun was the same one who'd been tracking the events along the San Andreas Fault. 'You make a habit of popping up in strange places, Mr Dobson,' she said.

'More of a business than a habit,' he said. 'I suppose you must be McFarlane, and you,' he flicked the gun at Jamie, 'do your parents know where you are, kid?'

'How did you find us?' demanded Elaine.

'Tracked you, it wasn't difficult – where's your friend, whatsisname . . . Stonegarden . . . where's he gone?'

'You came through the *door*!' interrupted Jamie, nursing his throbbing hand. 'How? How'd you know what to do?'

Dobson ignored him, retrieving the Colt as he quickly scanned the surrounding area. 'I said, where's your friend?'

'You want to know? Well you probably won't believe me, but I'll tell you anyway,' Elaine sat back on her heels. 'At this very moment he's trying to stop the state of California, no less, from being ripped apart by the mother and father of all earthquakes. OK?'

'Oh yeah?' sneered Dobson.

'You heard me,' said Elaine.

'You mean you guys aren't chasing down ancient artefacts?'

'No.'

'Well I'll be a monkey's uncle . . .' Dobson shook his head, half smiling. 'Let me get this straight – you know who I am, but you *don't* know anything else . . . who I work for, what I'm doing?'

'Don't know and right this minute I couldn't care less,' said Elaine. 'But then I get the impression that *you* don't have the slightest idea where you are or what you're dealing with either . . . am I right, Dobson?'

'Exactly where I am doesn't matter.' He kept them both covered as he stuck the Colt down the back of his jeans. 'I know I'm in the past and *that's* what counts – it's going to really make my employer's day when I get back and tell him about this.'

'This is a bigger deal than just collecting antiques!'

'Cut out the hysterics, McFarlane – this is the deal of a *lifetime*, and I don't want it getting messed up,' said Dobson. 'So just tell me where Stonegarden is . . .'

Once Red had handed over the small leather pouch things took a completely different turn. The old medicine man had shaken out on to his hand a small carved wooden figure, smooth with age, and stared at it for a long time, turning it over and over.

'My work,' he said at last. 'Where did you get it?'

'It has been in my family for four generations,' said Red. 'You will give it to my great grandfather's father.'

Silver Heart turned and walked back towards his teepee. 'You come with me,' he said, 'we have much to talk about.'

Inside the tent the air was laced with the aromatic smoke from a small fire at its centre. Silver Heart motioned for the women and children in there already to leave and sat down, cross-legged, on the hide-covered floor. 'Join me,' he said to Red and the five other people who had come in with him.

Time seemed to pass excruciatingly slowly; food and drink was brought in as Red was questioned by Silver Heart about who he was and where he came from. The old man could not believe he was talking to someone from the distant future – why should he? If Red had appeared more ghost-like it might have been easier for him to accept what was the wild truth – that this was no spirit walking in the hard world of Man, this was an unborn . . . *one who had yet to be.*

In the end, with the evidence of the wooden talisman in his grip, Silver Heart allowed that *maybe* Red was who he said he was, and came from where he said he came from. 'But why,' he then asked, 'did you come here?'

Red had been waiting for this moment; for him, he knew, the battle of words was about to start. 'You have been talking to the Great Earth Spirit,' he said, 'and your words have been heard where I come from. I am here to ask you to stop.'

'I cannot stop,' said Silver Heart. 'The Indian Nation lies bleeding on the Plains and I have to do what I can to halt the white man before it dies.'

'It doesn't die. I am here to show you that.'

This stopped the old man for a moment; he looked round at the warriors in the teepee and Red saw there was a silent agreement that what he'd said made sense.

Then Silver Heart smiled. 'But what if *you* are part of the Great Evil we are fighting?'

There was a murmur of approval, and Red could feel all eyes were on him. He felt completely out of his depth and wished more than anything that he could ask Simeon for advice – what to say, what to do next. His uncle had assumed that giving Silver Heart the talisman would make everything all right, but the shaman was still deeply suspicious of him. Somehow he had to convince the man to listen to him . . . somehow he had to find the right words.

Red took a deep breath. 'Tell me what you *think* you are doing,' he said.

'I am pleading with the Great Spirit to use the powers of the earth in *our* favour,' said Silver Heart, raising his voice, 'to bring down fire and torment on the white man – and my voice *will* be heard!'

'Is it working?' asked Red.

Silver Heart looked him through slitted eyes, his thin lips drawn tight. 'These things take time.'

'No!' Red almost shouted. 'Your voice *has* been heard, but not *here*! Your magic is out of control, Silver Heart, it's running wild – what you have done is like dropping a stone in a pond, but the waves are being felt far, far away. Believe me, if you carry on with what you're doing, nothing will happen here but it will tear *my* world apart.'

'You dare insult me?'

The atmosphere inside the teepee was charged, like just before a bad storm, and Red knew he was in trouble; then, from the back of his mind, he heard the whisper of a phrase Simeon had often used. He grabbed it like the drowning man he was, and repeated it.

'Only Earth Maker can create anything perfect, Silver Heart,' he said.

A look of stunned surprise spread over the old man's face and Red could hear murmured comments coming from the warriors. He carried on staring straight at the shaman and waited for him to say something. And waited.

Finally Silver Heart spread out his hands. 'What you say is true, and I should not have forgotten it,' he said, nodding. 'These are desperate times and I have not been careful . . . it seems I may have misused the powers I have been given.'

'Not mis*used*, more misdirected.'

'A mistake, whichever way you describe it,' said Silver Heart. 'And what you are telling me is that, whatever I do, our battle is lost.'

'We still survive, Silver Heart – I am living proof of that.' Red stood up and turned around to let everyone see him. 'In my time some of us still believe what you believe.'

'That is something . . .'

Dobson was going to get nasty, thought Jamie; the more Elaine insisted that Red wasn't off getting stuff to take back to the present, the more threatening he got. Still kneeling on the ground, he tried to think of something he could do to divert Dobson's attention, but the throbbing in his hand made it difficult to concentrate . . . and then it gave him an idea.

Elaine was to his left, Dobson in front and slightly to his right – it just might work. Groaning loud and agonizingly Jamie closed his eyes, clutched his 'wounded' hand and collapsed in a heap.

'You must've broken something when you kicked him,' he heard Elaine cry out. 'He's fainted!'

Through half-closed eyes Jamie saw Dobson, a puzzled look on his face, drop his guard and lean forward to peer at him. Now was his only chance to see if he was as fit as he liked to think he was.

With a piercing, high-pitched scream Jamie twisted himself over on his shoulder and struck out wildly with his legs. But the satisfying thud of his heavy leather boot hitting Dobson never came, and thumping back on the ground he looked up to find the snub grey nose of his automatic an inch from his nose.

'Try that again, kid,' hissed Dobson, 'and you're dead – now get back on your knees and stay there!'

Jamie, shaken and panting, picked himself up and stumbled over to where Elaine was still squatting; he'd blown it, only succeeding in making Dobson even madder than he was before. The man was standing in front of them looking fit to spit, and Jamie saw him raise his gun and point it at them.

'I've *had* it with you two,' he snarled. 'I'm gonna . . .'

But they never got to find out what he was going to do. There was a strange fluttering whisper in the air above their heads and the next thing they knew, Dobson was screaming and grabbing at an arrow that had gone through his shoulder and was sticking out the other side. For a moment neither of them moved, stunned by what had happened, then Elaine leapt to her feet and lunged for the gun he'd dropped. Getting up to follow her, Jamie looked over his shoulder to where the arrow had come from.

'Boots?' he whispered.

CHAPTER TWENTY-TWO

Timeline: Sunday, early afternoon

From out of the trees Boots Franklin and Tin-can Charley appeared, Boots with another arrow already fitted to his bow.

'They've come back, Elaine!' said Jamie.

'Their timing's perfect,' she replied, standing well out of kicking range with Dobson's automatic held steadily in both hands. Pointing at his chest.

'Gimme a break, McFarlane,' Dobson grunted, his bloody left hand holding his shoulder. 'Get this thing outta me!'

'All in good time,' she replied. 'Right now I'd trust you about as much as I would a rattlesnake.'

Boots and Tin-can came padding quietly into the campsite. 'OK?' asked Boots, Tin-can moving behind Dobson.

Jamie nodded. 'Thanks,' he said.

'What are you going to do to me?' Dobson's eyes flicked up at Boots.

'Nothing *like* what I figure you were planning for us,' said Elaine.

'D'you think we ought to go and get some help?' Jamie saw that the colour had drained out of Dobson's face. 'I know Red told us to stay here, but . . .'

'I think you're right, Jamie, time to take a walk.'

Red was exhausted. He seemed to have been talking for hours non-stop, one minute on the verge of convincing Silver Heart to stop what he was doing, the next back in the middle of an endless argument. He was beginning to lose his patience.

But Red knew that this was how it must be done; every facet of the situation had to be looked at, explored and discussed in mind-numbing detail. That was the way. The trouble was, apart from the talisman Simeon had given him, he couldn't prove what he was saying was the truth – and without proof, there was no reason on earth, so it seemed, for Silver Heart to believe him.

Then a warrior slipped quietly into the teepee and knelt behind Silver Heart, whispering in his ear. The old man frowned and looked over at Red.

'We have visitors,' he said, getting slowly to his feet.

Jamie could see the growing crowd of people at the edge of the encampment, although all he could hear was Dobson's muttered complaints as Boots and Tin-can Charley helped him walk through the long grass. Elaine was acting as an armed rear guard.

Boots and Tin-can hadn't wanted to come to the encampment, but whatever it was that had brought the two of them back in the first place (a sense of honour? wondered Jamie) had in the end also overcome their fear of Silver Heart. Using a mixture of sign language and a few scattered words, Jamie told the two Nez Percés what he wanted and finally they'd set off on foot.

Now they were nearly there.

Up ahead he could see expressions on individual faces, detail on clothing; he felt exposed at the front of this strange-looking, rag-tag group and realized his mouth was dry while the rest of him sweated. What he would do for a can of soda.

Ahead, right in front of him, he saw the line of watchers part and an old, white-haired man walked through the gap, followed by someone covered in dark markings . . . Red! Jamie almost let out a yell of delight, but thought better of it and carried on walking.

'You handing me over or something?' grumbled Dobson; each step was obviously causing him pain.

'No, we're just trying to get your shoulder fixed,' replied Jamie. 'Or would you rather we left the arrow in there and you bled to death?'

They were now only twenty, thirty metres away and Jamie didn't know whether to stop or carry on. He looked at Red and saw him beckon. 'Time to put the gun away, Elaine?'

'Yeah, not much he can do now, I guess,' she said, snapping on the safety catch and tucking it underneath her shirt and in the back of her jeans.

'What should I do – shake his hand?' Jamie called back, noticing the old man lean over and say something to Red.

'S'pose so.'

'Whatever you decide to do, get on with it,' grunted Dobson. 'My whole damn shoulder's on fire . . .'

Jamie walked on, aware of the long grass brushing against his legs, aware of all the eyes watching him and the disconcerting silence that had fallen all around them. He made straight for the old man – it could, he thought, only be Silver Heart – and put out his hand in greeting. 'Hello,' he said.

Silver Heart took his hand and held it. 'Jay-mee?' he said, a question in his voice; Jamie nodded and Silver Heart swung his other hand out and smiled.

'He's welcoming you to the camp,' said Red. 'I think you guys may just have solved my problem . . .'

The next hour or so went by in a whirl. Dobson was taken to a teepee where Silver Heart himself supervised the tending of his wound; Jamie and Elaine sat and watched from the sidelines as the arrow's shaft was broken and then pulled out of his shoulder. Once his heavily blood-soaked jacket and shirt had been removed, Dobson looked about as white as a white man could before he went green.

Silver Heart made a hot poultice from herbs and leaves and applied it to both sides of the cleaned wound then, leaving the bandaging to one of the women, he came over to speak to Red. Jamie listened to the discussion, wondering what was being said; he watched the old man point to Dobson's leather jacket, his Nike trainers and his chrome wrist-watch, saw him frowning and shaking his head.

'What d'you think's going on?' he whispered to Elaine.

'Your guess is as good as mine,' she said, 'but *I'd* say he's having something of a reality problem.'

'Huh?'

'Remember what Red said when we got here? That we might just have solved his problem?' Jamie nodded. 'Well I think that whatever Red's been telling him, Dobson's arrival has convinced Silver Heart it's true.'

Jamie was fiddling with a small straw figure he'd found on the ground when he saw Red coming over to them. 'What's happening?' he asked as he ushered them out of the teepee.

'We've done it,' he said.

'Done what?'

'He's agreed to stop calling on the spirits . . . who *is* this man anyway? Where'd he come from?' Red cocked his head in Dobson's direction.

Jamie looked over at him, lying on a fur skin, his shoulder bandaged up, and he heard Elaine explain what had happened.

'We have to go,' Red said when she'd finished her story. 'We mustn't stay here too long, especially with this man – we'll move out soon.'

'How's Dobson going to make it?' asked Jamie. 'He still looks pretty bad.'

'Don't worry,' grinned Red, 'he's lost a lot of blood, but he'll be fine.'

Leaving Dobson, Red took them over to another teepee

where Boots and Tin-can were waiting. Silver Heart and a group of warriors joined them and they all sat round in a circle. The atmosphere was tense, and in a weird way it seemed to Jamie as if he and Elaine were being treated as if they weren't actually there; it made him feel nervous but he realized that their hosts felt the same way as well; while he was in a foreign land – a foreign *time*, even – they were looking at people whom they knew shouldn't exist. Ghosts from the future.

Watching the proceedings, Jamie suddenly realized he was still holding the tiny straw doll in his hands. It occurred to him that it would be perfect to take back as Teejay's souvenir; when the time was right, he thought, slipping it into his shirt pocket, he'd ask Red if it was OK to do that.

A moment later Silver Heart was getting to his feet and appeared to be giving orders to the men around him.

'Red?' queried Elaine

'Time to go,' he replied. 'Come on . . .'

'What was that last bit all about?' asked Jamie.

'Nothing, really,' muttered Red. 'Just our way of finishing things off.'

There was something in the way he answered that didn't quite ring true, but Jamie knew he'd have to keep any suspicions to himself. Things were beginning to happen, and at speed. Following Red and the two guides, Elaine and Jamie found themselves back out on the edge of the encampment where Dobson was waiting for them.

He was lying on hides that had been stretched across an

A-shaped frame of poles attached to a horse, and he still looked very pale and was covered with a blanket. 'What is *that*?' said Jamie.

'It's called a travois,' Red told him. 'It's the only way to travel around here – if you can't walk or ride.'

It had been a subdued farewell, Silver Heart solemnly shaking hands with all of them, even Boots and Tincan. And then they were off, trudging back across the grassland to their campsite. It was, Jamie thought, a bit of an anti-climax, but endings so very often were – no big fanfare, cheers or shouts. From the tribe's point of view they were probably glad to see the back of them, to forget they'd ever had these particular visitors.

Jamie looked back once, when they were about half way to the rise, and was almost shocked to see that no-one had stayed to watch them. It was as if they'd never been there.

No-one spoke very much, not even Dobson. He seemed to still be in some pain, but some colour had come back to his face. Jamie fell in next to the travois and, for want of anything better to do, eventually struck up a conversation.

'Why's he do it?' he asked.

'Who?'

'Your boss,' said Jamie. 'Why spend all that money chasing after stuff . . . who is he anyway?'

Dobson looked at Jamie for a long time as if weighing up the pros and cons of answering his question. And then he began to talk. He told him he worked for someone called Cletus Whelan IV, which, he was sure, would mean absolutely nothing to Jamie because that was exactly how Mr Whelan liked it. Whelan, he explained, was a ludicrously wealthy guy who'd become totally obsessed with acquiring things from the outer reaches of myth, magic and science: ancient books, the bones of saints, bits of UFOs – basically the weirder the better.

Dobson said he'd worked for Whelan for a couple of years now, hired as a kind of Mr Fix-it and told to set up a secret network of agents. And that was how they'd found out about the California business – all the strange, unexplained things that were appearing out of nowhere.

'So why all the secrecy?' asked Jamie.

'The government's on to this thing as well, though not for the same reasons as Whelan . . .'

'The Special Scientific Office?' said Jamie.

'Yeah, them . . . and Whelan's paranoid they'll take all his precious things away, and he also thinks people will try and get stuff before him, or charge more if they know it's him buying, etcetera, etcetera,' said Dobson. 'Actually, paranoid doesn't really do the man justice . . . he's probably certifiable.'

'Was it your people who broke into my house?' asked Elaine. She'd heard the two of them talking and had fallen back to join in.

Dobson nodded. 'The trouble with working for someone who's pathologically suspicious is that it rubs off; you end up having to think like they do to survive.

'The more I found out about you,' Dobson went on, 'the bigger the conspiracy theory I built up in my head; you hang around someone like Whelan long enough and there's no such thing as coincidence any more – especially when a reporter's involved.'

'So you tracked us to the valley and found the door,' said Elaine. 'That must've made you think . . . seeing our footsteps disappear into it, into nowhere – why did you follow us?'

'The thought of the bonus Whelan would give me when I came back,' said Dobson.

'You weren't frightened?' said Jamie. 'Didn't you know you could *die* going through one of those things?'

'I knew what to do – I'd seen one before. We got the conquistador on tape . . .'

'How come you knew where that was going to happen?' enquired Elaine.

'Oh, you wouldn't *believe* the technology money can buy these days,' smiled Dobson.

'You're a snake-in-the-grass, Dobson, smooth talking and silver-tongued,' Elaine said. 'Why should we believe you?'

'Yeah – who says you aren't FBI, CIA, or maybe even Mafia, on some oh-so-secret mission?' Jamie pointed at him.

'Believe what you like, both of you,' scowled Dobson, gritting his teeth as the travois bounced over a large bump, 'it's the truth.'

'Or as near as we'll ever get to it,' said Elaine.

CHAPTER TWENTY-THREE

Timeline: Sunday night
and Saturday morning, late

They stopped long enough at the camp for Red to clean himself in the stream while Elaine and Jamie tied the bed rolls. Boots and Tin-can, who'd left their mounts with the others, busied themselves getting the horses ready.

'Why aren't we staying here the night?' Jamie asked Red when he came back.

'We have to be gone by sunrise.'

'Gone from where?' said Elaine.

'This time.' Red shook water from his hair.

'Why?' asked Jamie.

'We just do,' replied Red. 'It's the way it has to be.'

It took quite a while longer to make the journey back because of the travois and the hours seemed to drag by. It soon got dark and there was nothing to look at until the moon came up and even then the world was black and white, but mostly black.

The slow pace and the cool night meant that they had to wrap Dobson in their bed rolls and wear all the clothes they had. Jamie had almost fallen asleep twice by the time

Red called a halt and was numb with cold as he slipped to the ground.

'We have to walk from here,' Red told them. 'The travois won't make it. Boots and Tin-can'll help me with Dobson. Leave everything you don't need here, best we can do in the way of payment.'

Jamie watched as Red took off his holster and gave it to Boots. Was this whole time thing just one great big circle? he wondered. Would that gun be back at Simeon's house when he got there? Jamie was too tired to follow the confusion of this train of thought and went over to where Tin-can was standing and handed over the reins to his horse.

With excruciating slowness they made their way up to where the doorway was. Although Dobson was still weak from the loss of blood it didn't stop him from being in a foul mood after the journey, and Jamie was surprised by how nervous Red appeared to be. And then, as they came down a narrow pathway, Jamie spotted it – half-hidden by a rocky overhang the door shimmered in the pearly light. In his mind's eye there was a big flashing neon sign above it saying 'EXIT'.

'How's Dobson going to get through, Red?' asked Elaine.

Boots and Tin-can had left the moment the door came into view, disappearing into the night, eyes wide with fear, and leaving the four of them alone. Looking around, Jamie thought he could just make out a faint pink glow to the east. Dawn.

'I'll be fine,' growled Dobson. 'Come on, let's get outta this place!'

'We'll walk single-file,' said Red, chewing his lip. 'I'll go first. Dobson, you hold tight on my shoulders – Elaine, Jamie, follow behind. We've got to hurry now!'

There he was again, being edgy and uptight . . . but why? Everything *seemed* to be going fine. Puzzled, Jamie wondered what could be worrying him but Red wasn't hanging around for a chat; helping Dobson down to the doorway he stood squarely in front of it.

'Hands on my shoulders, Dobson,' he said.

'Don't need telling twice,' came the curt reply as Elaine got close behind him, and Red began to walk. They were going home.

Jamie moved into the shiny, hissing door, eyes firmly fixed on Elaine's back. Through the agitated, roiling air he went . . . going back and forward at the same time, it occurred to him. He was concentrating so hard on not touching the sides that he didn't notice the light change. So when he came out the other side, into blindingly bright daylight, for one long, horrible moment he thought he'd made a mistake and had died.

'Stay right where you are,' he heard a voice he didn't recognize say. 'Put your hands in the air and then don't move!'

Jamie blinked, his eyes hurting from the light, and did as he was told. What were they – whoever 'they' were – doing, shining a *spot*light on them? he thought.

'That you, Cardwell?' he heard Dobson say. 'Nice of you to come and pick us up.'

Slowly Jamie was able to make out where he was. They were back in the valley and it was daytime! Squinting he saw the others about a metre in front of him, hands also in the air; ranged in a semi-circle around them were a dozen or so men in combat gear, weapons pointing at them. To add to the air of complete unreality, behind the armed men, Jamie could see a lone trail bike propped on its stand.

'Long time, no see, Dobson,' said one of the men, walking forward. He had a pistol in his hand and was wearing mirrored sunglasses and some kind of head gear with a tiny microphone looping in front of his face. 'Move away from that thing now, slowly forward,' he said, motioning them to come towards him.

'Nice of you to look after my bike, Gene,' said Dobson. 'You been waiting all this time for us to come back?'

'All what time, Dobson?' Jamie could see the man's brow furrow. 'You just went, maybe ten . . . fifteen minutes ago – what happened to you?'

'I went, must be twenty-four *hours* ago. What day is it?'

'Saturday.'

The four of them looked at each other, bemused, bewildered and stunned. *Saturday afternoon?* What had happened to Sunday? If what this man was saying was true they'd walked back into the same day they'd left . . . looped right back to where they'd started. Jamie shook his head – no harder to believe, he supposed, than anything else that'd happened.

'Who are you?' said Elaine. 'How'd you know we'd be here – were you *following* us?'

'No, him,' the man, Cardwell, nodded at Dobson. 'We saw him disappear and were waiting to see what happened when you all came back out.'

'You closing Whelan down?' queried Dobson. 'He's not going to be very happy about that.'

'We're taking over,' said Cardwell. 'This is all too serious for a fruitcake like Whelan to be involved in. We've cordoned the whole area off and we'll be thoroughly investigating this thing you've discovered.'

'You'll be lucky,' said Red.

'What d'you mean?' Cardwell turned to look at him.

'It's the only one there is, and it's shutting down.'

Jamie frowned. The only door? Closing down? What was Red on about? And then behind him he heard a strange rushing noise, like a bath running out; glancing over his shoulder he saw the shimmering air of the doorway was now vibrating very fast and visibly shrinking by the second. He could see Red smiling in an odd, almost relieved way and suddenly previously meaningless pieces of conversation and out-of-character behaviour all made sense.

'Silver Heart?' he whispered, and Red's smile got broader. So *that* was why he'd been so insistent that they get out before dawn – it was a deadline and somehow Silver Heart had managed to close the door. For ever.

This time it was the turn of Cardwell and his men to be confused and baffled. Like sugar dissolving in hot water, Simeon's door was disappearing . . . and then it was gone. Not with a bang or a whimper, just gone, like it had never ever existed. Jamie could sense their disappointment and wondered what was going to happen next. Cardwell was the first to snap back into action.

'Whatever it was has closed down,' he said, head down and talking into his microphone. 'We've lost it – kick in phase two and let's move these people out of here, on the double.'

'Hold on,' said Elaine. 'I'm not going *any*where until you tell me what's going on! Who are you guys?'

Jamie spoke without even thinking. 'Special Scientific Office,' he said, and saw Cardwell lock his gaze on to him; somewhere in the distance he thought he could hear at least one helicopter. 'The other people out there looking, Elaine.'

'You might just be too sharp for your own good, kid,' said Dobson.

Elaine had obviously picked up the sound of the rotors as well. 'You got plans to whip us all off somewhere for a bit of brainwashing?' she said. 'You know, like you must've done to all those people from the park – that was no way a pack of wild dogs, was it?'

'Wild dogs?' laughed Dobson. 'My informant said that was a herd of *dinosaurs*, McFarlane.'

'Four, actually,' said Cardwell, 'and we prefer to call it deep hypnosis.'

From over the lip of the valley Jamie saw two large beetle-like helicopters rise into the clear blue sky. For the first time since this whole thing had started he began to feel *very* scared. What was going to happen to them? Where were they going to be taken? Would these people *really* brainwash them? And then Red started talking.

'It's all over,' he said. 'No more breakthoughs, everything back to normal . . . finished. Nothing else'll happen.'

'Where've you four just been . . . through that doorway?'

'You wouldn't believe me if I told you,' said Red. 'So I won't, and neither will the others.'

They all looked at each other in silent agreement and Elaine relaxed slightly, folding her arms. 'This is what I think they call an impasse, Mr Cardwell,' she said. 'We won't tell you what *you* don't want *us* to tell other people – am I right?'

Cardwell pursed his lips. 'Looks that way.'

The two copters were getting louder and nearer and beginning to throw up small clouds of dust. 'So where do we go from here?' asked Elaine.

'We make a deal,' said Dobson. 'Gene's good at that, and it always involves signing some damn piece of official government paper – right, Gene? So let's do it and get the heck out of here and back to civilization!'

Simply put, the 'piece of official government paper' they'd signed had sworn them to absolute secrecy, on pain of all kinds of stuff, the least of which were fines and imprisonment. It was, thought, Jamie, a fairly useless thing to put your name to because no-one would ever believe what had happened to them anyway – especially as he didn't even know if *he* did. The only people he'd be able to talk about it with were Elaine, Red and grumpy old Charles Dobson. But he had a feeling he'd probably never see him again.

Dobson had been put in one copter and flown off, presumably to a hospital, while he, Red and Elaine had waited next to the other one. All three of them were exhausted, tired to the bone, and they still had to get home; Jamie felt jet-lagged and all he wanted was a hot shower and his own bed.

When Gene Cardwell reappeared he told them what was going to happen. Red's truck, he said, was being driven back to Simeon's where the copter would take him; Elaine and Jamie would fly on to Santa Monica Airport and a car would then take them each home.

'But my car's out at Red's place,' said Elaine.

'Simeon and me'll bring it back tomorrow,' Red told her. 'He'll want to see you.'

'Your uncle's already signed his papers,' said Cardwell, 'and remember Ms McFarlane, breathe *one* word, write a *single* paragraph and we'll be down on you like a ton of bricks.'

'I couldn't sell this story to even the *wackiest* supermarket tabloid, and you know it,' she replied. 'Which gives me a bit of a problem when it comes to telling my boss what I've been up to these last few days.'

'Research,' said Jamie. 'Isn't that what you usually tell him?'

'You'll make a great reporter yet, Jamie,' smiled Elaine, climbing up into the copter.

Following her up the steps Jamie felt something in his shirt pocket. The straw doll. Teejay's souvenir – the only proof he'd ever have that, for a day, he'd walked the plains of North America with the likes of Boots Franklin and Tin-can Charley, and shaken hands with the most powerful medicine man that ever lived.

And helped stop an earthquake, of course.